BEST S&M

III

Still More Extreme Stories of Still More Extreme Sex

Edited By M.Christian

Best S & M Erotica III: Still More Extreme Stories of Still More Extreme Sex

M.Christian (editor)

Published by Logical-Lust, copyright 2010

ISBN: 978-1905091-63-8
Paperback version
Published by Logical-Lust Publications © 2010

Cover image by Helen E. H. Madden, pixelarcana.com
© Logical-Lust Publications 2010

CONTENTS

Introduction: "More of the Best ..."

How is a writer like a masochist?

Believe it or not, there actually is an answer. It's not like Carroll's "How is a raven like a writing desk?" riddle, which doesn't have one.

But before I deliver the punch line, let me welcome you to *Best S/M Erotica Vol 3: Still More Extreme Stories of Still More Extreme Sex*. As with the previous volumes, I tried to pick stories that reflect not just traditional S/M, meaning sado-masochism or pain-for-pleasure, but also to cover the very wide-ranging world of sex based on power exchange. S/M is weird that way. No, I don't mean that as a judgment call—I'm of the school that if it's consensual, it's okay—but, unlike other sexual themes, S/M can mean different things to different people.

So here, in these pages, you'll find light stories, dark stories, powerful stories, subtle stories, fierce stories, and even romantic stories—but all of them deal with the basic idea of consensually giving up, or taking, sexual power and control.

What really is odd about editing these books is how it makes me feel—and not in a sexual way. Sure, there's pleasure—if not joy—in finding stories that celebrate the widely varied dimensions of S/M and accomplish that very difficult task with style, beautiful language, fine characterization, and something more than merely sexual passion. But as a writer myself, this pleasure can sometimes be overshadowed by the disappointment I know all too well: the bad part of the job of editing an anthology that comes when you have to tell the folks who–for whatever reasons–didn't make the cut.

That's why, in a weirdly twisted way, being a writer can be like being a masochist. After all, what else would you call someone who has to get some kind of a pleasure out of a thankless job like writing, and submitting, stories?

Okay, that's a bit of a stretch–and a bad riddle–but it's my way of saying that I hope you enjoy this book. I think the writers have each done remarkable jobs of trying to show what S/M can be but also, and more importantly, done it with magnificent literary skill.

But that it's also important that you realize that they, and the people who didn't make the cut, deserve the highest praise any Master, or editor, can give to those who have submitted to them:

"You've done good."

– M.Christian, 2009

Mealtime Trappings

By
Craig J. Sorensen

Carefully rolled white napkins in polished silver rings were poised on opposite sides of the card table in the bedroom. Two matching vinyl chairs awaited; one would be used. Scents of a stir-fry filled the air. Matching purple silk short shorts and tiny camisole waited atop the satin comforter.

The light in the room across the way was on, so Ying dimmed her bedroom light as she entered the room. She set the dinner on the card table and went in the deepest corner where she quickly peeled off her sweats, and then smoothed the drizzle of sweat from her brow down her cheeks. The silk top fell like a stage curtain over her plump nipples.

She checked the clock as the shorts came to rest on her hips.

8:02. The action across the way had predictably begun.

Ying had dubbed him Jeremy for silly reasons. Though he was not a ringer for Jeremy Irons, the man across seemed forged from iron. He was short and muscular. He had a deep chin, a strong brow, and long, wild blonde hair. Despite his stout physique, he had strangely lithe ballerina moves. But what he did was not a dance.

Every Tuesday and Friday at 8:00 Jeremy entertained a guest of sorts.

Ying savored the cold vinyl of the chair and drizzled soy sauce from a crystal cruet across the rare prime rib, snow peas, and pearl onions over jasmine rice. She balanced antique carved ivory chopsticks and took a bite.

Jeremy was clad, shoulder to shank, in formfitting, gleaming black leather. A woman stood framed perfectly by his long window. She was dressed in skintight black cloth like a burglar. Jeremy wielded a riding crop. The thief remained still, her gloved hands neatly folded in front of her groin.

A few weeks prior, Ying had looked out her bedroom window to see a nude woman hanging from a hook deep in the room. She picked up her phone and pressed 9-1 and hovered over the 1 button. But the puzzling rapture on the woman's face, the deliberate presence of a hook mounted to the ceiling, punctuated by the fact the man was wearing carefully fitted, shiny leather convinced Ying to hang up and watch in growing fascination.

Tonight, Jeremy stripped the mask and the thief's long, bright red hair spilled out in random curls. Jeremy gripped her cheeks and spoke so close that it could have been a kiss.

Red shook her head softly as Jeremy grabbed her hair behind her skull and opened her throat. Ying felt a deep pulse in her belly remembering when Marvin Stack yanked her long black hair on the playground, followed by her sudden blinding anger as she punched him and knocked him on his ass, interrupting his career as a puller of girls' hair. But later, Ying had felt a strange curiosity at the sensations.

Jeremy forced his mouth over Red's.

Ying took another bite of her meal. Rules were rules. She could not join in until she had finished.

Jeremy engulfed Red's wrists in his left hand and bound them with plastic zip cuffs.

Ying savored how her pussy slid. She took another bite, and then another, and then finally stopped just short of shoveling like a longshoreman after a twelve-hour shift. She twirled her chopsticks over and under each other feigning patience.

Jeremy hung Red's wrists on the hook. The front of his pants filled.

Ying took another bite from her half-full plate. Her defiant hand dipped into her silk shorts and caressed the edge of her downy pubic hair. She returned the rogue hand back on the table and took two more fast bites.

Jeremy yanked the skin-tight top up Red's chest and groped her breasts harshly.

The weekend after she had first seen Jeremy and Red, Ying aggressively seduced her boyfriend Ronny. He seemed to like it as she pulled his stiffness from his pants. She tossed his balled up T-shirt toward the coffee table, covering the head of the gold Buddha.

Her fresh desires grew irresistible when she was fiercely turned on; it stood to reason that Ronny be the same. She took it further and squeezed his cock hard. "Ying! Ow!"

She crawled over his knee.

"What?"

"Spank me!" She lifted her short skirt and lowered her panties.

"Gawd Ying!" Ronny deflated like a clown's balloon after an incompetent attempt at an animal sculpture.

Jeremy peeled off Red's tight pants. He shoved one gloved hand down the front of her black G-string. Red began to writhe. He tugged her nipples hard with his other hand, and then circled her and pressed tight against her butt. Red's mouth gaped.

Ying quickly retrieved a pair of brown leather gloves from the closet, inhaled the last of her meal, and wiped her chin on her wrist just above the top of her glove.

Both rolled up napkins lay unmolested.

Jeremy pushed the back of Red's G-string down, and then spanked her butt hard. His other hand, still down the front, steadied her. He teased with little pats, and then sudden, powerful pops that Ying was sure she could hear.

The scrape of the glove's seam against Ying's clit made her gasp, but she knew that this time it would not be enough to just masturbate hard. She looked at her other gloved hand, and then out across the way as Jeremy swatted Red.

Ying's stomach turned over as she pulled her silk shorts down one hip and raised her hand. She'd never felt more than a playful swat.

Jeremy reached up, it seemed in slow motion, and Ying looked up at her hand. As his hand traveled down, Ying mimicked the stroke. A huge, almost orgasmic grunt from her own throat surprised Ying as the sting spread. Each time Jeremy swatted Red, Ying swatted herself as if she were doing a sound effect track for a movie.

It was most convincing.

The gloved fingers in her cunt slid like skates on ice.

Jeremy suddenly pulled Red's hands down from the hook and shoved her deep into the room. The bulge at the front of his pants was as sharp as a flagpole in shrink-wrap.

Ying gasped. "Please, please take off your pants, Jeremy." Her fingers continued to pump and she spanked herself a couple more times for good measure.

Jeremy walked deeper into the room.

Ying knew the show was over. She raced to the bed and fell face down. Her legs sprawled wide. She alternated hands, spanking and masturbating until her waist clenched like a vise. She stopped breathing as a great weight in her waist expelled in an orgasm like she'd never felt, one that gave her goose bumps on her skull. She laughed convulsively.

She was embarrassed, defiled, powerful, excited.

Her butt felt like festive champagne, only better.

For the next show Ying upped the ante. A new outfit shimmered atop her bed like fresh fallen snow on a sunny winter morning. She dimmed the lights and stepped into the depth of the room and undressed. Just the scent of the new leather made her moist.

As she stood nude, the sight of her shiny skin in the mirror reminded her of a game she'd once played with her Barbie and her older brother's G.I. Joe: she bound Joe into a pink Barbie chair with black twist ties. She hadn't thought about what Barbie might do to her quarry. The possibilities made her dizzy. But her brother caught her, called her "freak," and liberated Joe. The fantasy was left to germinate like an acorn in the depths of a lotus garden. Joe escaped to the safety of hard-core hand-to-hand with his nemesis Cobra.

The elastic laces down the legs of her pants stretched to accommodate her shapely thighs and calves, while clinging perfectly to her trim knees and ankles. The lace-up corset formed perfectly around her breasts and squeezed her ribs tightly. She topped the outfit off with elbow-length white leather gloves.

The white outfit underscored her short-bobbed silky black hair and deep olive skin. A strip of her dark stomach incised the corset and pants. She'd never felt sexier.

Across the way, Jeremy circled Red who was in a crisp business suit, but he was not in his customary leather. His tan uniform was nondescript. He leaned his head to one side and looked in Red's down-turned eyes. Both seemed uncharacteristically fidgety. Red obediently took something off after each noncommittal swat from Jeremy until she stood in her underwear. She reached for the clasp of her bra between her breasts.

Jeremy shook his head and gripped her hand. Any hint of menace drained away as he spoke gently to Red. Her head tilted like a curious puppy. He held the riding crop, handle out, like the careful presentation of a stiletto.

She cradled it like a long-stemmed rose.

Ying spread her legs and crushed the seam at the crotch to her hard clit.

Jeremy went to the hook and grabbed it. Red gently tapped the riding crop into her hand. Ying defied the empty plate rule and squeezed her hand into her tight pants. "Go for it!"

Red dropped the crop and folded her arm over the front of her bra. She shook her head and backed away. Jeremy seemed angry at first, and then appeared to plead; his iron suddenly drooped as if it had been returned to the forging fire.

Red quickly put on her blouse and pinched it at the clasp of her bra. She grabbed the skirt and disappeared from view.

Jeremy raced after her.

Ying sat, legs spread, hand limp in her tight leather pants. Her other hand dangled like the motionless hook in the room across the way.

The two now were in his living room. Ying rushed down the hall to get a better view as if her presence might encourage a favorable outcome.

Red shoved the tail of her blouse into her skirt and Jeremy took one of her hands in his. It looked like he might drop to one knee in a cliché marriage proposal. He stroked her knuckles and continued to speak. Red was motionless, absorbing. Jeremy bit his lip and looked outside.

Strange, but Ying had never seen either of them look outside. She suddenly realized how bright her living room was, and her gleaming leather outfit must look like sun-drenched binocular lenses in a war movie. She jumped from view, and then peered around the curtain after a few moments. Jeremy was focused on motionless Red again.

Red's head shook side to side. Jeremy said something, and Red eased her hand from his and walked toward the front door of his apartment. She held up her hand to stop him from following. As the door shut behind her, his shoulders slumped. He disappeared from view.

Ying felt a letdown deeper than the day G.I. Joe got away. But after a few minutes, she felt a strange wave of relief. She'd already sacrificed her relationship with Ronnie when she tried a second time to get him to spank her.

Ying rushed to her dim bedroom, closed the curtains, changed into safe sweats, dismantled her impromptu table and chairs, and relegated all the accoutrement of the meal-time trappings into the corner of her closet. She ate her cold meal in the dining room, staring blankly at the nondescript painting of a field of daisies on the wall.

Ying unzipped her tan skirt and reached deep into her closet. She brushed smooth leather and the scent filled the air. "No reason I can't enjoy how it feels." Ying had spent a small fortune on it. She'd not had sex or even masturbated in weeks, since seeing Red walk out on Jeremy. She was starved to feel sexy.

There was a sense of comfort even well worn sweats could not rival as the white cocoon encased her nude body. The curtains in her bedroom hadn't been open in weeks. What was wrong with being seen, looking as sexy as she had ever felt? She opened them.

The light in the bedroom across the way was on, and she realized it was 8:00. There was a brief twinge of hope that Jeremy had reconciled with Red, and that their passion play would be in summer reruns. But Jeremy plodded past the window dressed in faded jeans and a loose sweatshirt. Suddenly his head reappeared in the window like a cartoon double take. Ying cocked to leap from view. She froze and slowly hooked her thumbs in the tops of her pants, anchoring so she couldn't defensively cover.

Jeremy pressed to the glass.

Ying gripped her hips in pseudo-confidence.

He gave her a "thumbs up." They remained locked like a game of "chicken" before Jeremy disappeared into his room, and then jumped back into view. He held up one finger. Ying nodded and said, "I'll wait." He disappeared again and, after a few minutes, reappeared in tight black cloth pants, a thin black long sleeved shirt, black gloves, and a mask like Red had worn. The pants did nothing to camouflage a growing, needful bulge. He waited, and Ying gave a "thumbs up." He held up a small bag, and then he put the riding crop inside it.

Blood squeezed up Ying's jugular like Stooges in a doorframe. She nodded and Jeremy disappeared from view. In moments, a dark figure moved along the bushes between the two buildings and rounded the corner.

A wisp of air under her front door announced the opening of the main entryway to her apartment building. Fear, titillation, and excitement supercharged her. She turned off the lights, opened the lock and slid the chain free of its channel, and waited behind the door. It seemed forever until it slowly opened. The crack of light shot a long V-shaped male shadow deep into the living room. Ying held her breath when he paused on the threshold.

The thief finally began to feel his way into the room. He was even thicker than he appeared, and he smelled so clean and masculine. Chills ran up and down Ying's spine. She worried he would turn on her like a rottweiler. She worried he wouldn't. He walked with a strange gait, arms swinging like urgent bell clappers. She realized he was offering her his hands. She accepted and twisted his arm behind his back.

He held his free hand up. "I give up! Let me go!" The more his deep voice trembled, the more the moisture between Ying's legs flowed.

After an awkward pause, she forced a contrived Chinese accent in a husky voice she thought might sound exotic and menacing. "Why you come here?"

"Please don't...don't..." He remained still as a frightened deer. Even through her gloves she could feel his rapid pulse. "I'll do...anything."

"You strip."

An approving sigh like a soft orgasm issued from his body. She released his hand and he obediently pulled the shirt over his broad chest. The coat of golden hair made her sigh; she loved hairy men. She fought back into character. "Pants too!"

His Adam's apple jumped as if he were swallowing a rabbit. Ying slapped his butt softly but made a surprisingly loud snap. She opened her mouth to apologize but he filled the void first. "Yes ma'am!"

She looked down his body, but her eyes moved back up to his face in embarrassment. She traced his bicep delicately. He seemed to melt. She pulled the mask from his face. His long curly blonde hair spilled like a waterfall. She laced her fingers in his curls playfully. They were even softer than hers and smelled sweet. She stroked for a time, wondering if he might call it off. She recalled that feeling from the playground.

She squeezed a fistful of the downy gold, and then yanked. "Ow, fuck!" It burned from his throat. She was stunned at the rage in his eyes, how huge his muscles flexed and how big his clenched fists were. Ying's heart beat double time and she released his hair. She held up her hands apologetically.

He held up his hand and mouthed "it's okay." He went limp, his mouth gaped as if to submit. She slowly opened her mouth over his and pushed her tongue in. Jeremy moaned so deeply that his voice resonated in her belly. It was approval, it was submission. Moisture spread down Ying's thigh.

She pulled his tiny underwear down to expose his butt. "Hands."

"Please, ma'am, allow me to make it up to you."

It became easier. "You will make up to me! Hands!" He crossed them in the small of his back. Her small fingers struggled to circle his thick wrists. She swatted his ass almost delicately with the other hand. He arched his butt, eager for more.

She snapped a bit harder and his mouth gaped. She suddenly popped him hard and he mouthed "oh yes." She teased and rubbed gently, and then snapped him hard when he seemed to relax, like he'd done to Red. She released his hands and stroked his hardness. "Why leave these on?"

"Sorry, mistress!" He pushed the underwear down and stepped out, and then raised his hands over his head like a prisoner of war.

She tugged him close by the base of his burgundy-red cock. "Name?"

"Gerry." It was eerily close to Jeremy.

"You learn lesson?"

"Yes, mistress."

It's okay, no harm done. These reflex words looped in her head. She forced out the word, "Liar." His eyes closed like an orgasm was mounting. Adrenaline coated Ying's mouth. She swallowed hard. "I tie you to bed."

He turned his head toward her. For a moment she wondered if he would. He whispered, "Oh God yes, ma'am."

Ying tied Gerry spread-eagled with twine from the kitchen. His cock issued from his crotch like a 1960's rocket ship on the launch pad. She wanted to do everything, but she hadn't advanced much beyond Barbie versus Joe days. She froze.

"I could, pleasure you, ma'am...with my mouth."

The offer released the vapor lock. She grabbed his cock again. "No. I take what I want. You not let go."

"Yes ma'am."

Ying peeled down her white leather pants and straddled him. As she pumped him hard, his head rolled like an encroaching orgasm. She slapped his face. But hitting his face was much different than his butt, and she wondered if it might affect him like tugging his hair. She covered her mouth. "Oh, Gerry I'm so – " Her accent was gone.

He grinned, and then looked scared.

She resumed slowly and read his face and body. Each time he grew toward orgasm, she stopped. Occasionally, she slapped his face and returned to her accent. "You come when I say."

"Oh, yes, mistress."

She left his needful cock smoldering on the launch pad and straddled his mouth. She gripped his skull tight to her cunt and ground the peak of her pubic bone to his nose. She stopped feeling like she was watching herself from a distant vantage. His long tongue traced her slit. "Harder. Flick faster.

Not so long there! Inside now!" He followed every instruction to the letter.

But it was not his adherence to instruction that led Ying to the first orgasm she'd had from a lover's mouth; it was the control that spurred her as she screamed out. She stripped the rest of her leather and slid down to his rod again, pressed her feet in his knees and split them wider. She whispered in his ear, "Your body now mine."

"Yes. Yes, mistress."

"You say that so I let you come?" She savored his chest hairs.

"No, please leave me unsatisfied. Let me prove myself."

"Now you come!"

"No, please, mistress!"

Gerry's bound body writhed. He grunted and groaned and tried to ease away from her, but she ground her hips harder and shoved her tongue deep in his ear. "Come now, fucking pig!" His orgasm blasted like a fire hose and the grunt from his throat seemed to shake the room. She couldn't believe what she called him.

Gerry let out a deep, strange laugh. Ying giggled in reply.

They lay panting for a time until she whispered without the accent, "My name is Ying."

"You're fucking awesome, Ying!"

She stroked his face, and then released and embraced his warm, furry body.

Gerry was cupped to Ying's back, the head of his hard cock fused to her tailbone, when she awoke. He gently stroked her upper arm. She slid beneath him and spread her legs. He kissed down her neck along her breasts. He dipped between her legs and ate her gently, very differently than she had instructed. It made her ascend more slowly, even so, for the second time in her life, she had an orgasm from a lover's mouth.

He triumphantly crawled up between her legs and touched the tip of his cock to her pussy lips.

Ying nodded her approval and he descended into her.

Despite his bulk, Gerry moved delicately. He kissed her neck and she opened it so he could bite. She wanted to feel the full might that had punished her via remote control; Red's rapture was something she coveted. He kissed more gently. She twirled one of the strands of twine, still tied on each corner of her bed, in her hand. "You know, I used to watch...Tuesdays and Fridays."

He nodded. "I know. Um...good peripheral vision."

Ying laughed, and then tilted her head down subserviently. "Sometimes I want..."

His expression shifted immediately to the one she had seen in his last night with Red.

She stroked her hands delicately in his chest hair. "To be made love to gently."

"Oh, of course." He made love to her slowly, sweetly, reverently.

Tuesdays and Fridays Ying and Gerry shared meals in their respective bedrooms via remote control. Gerry the remote; Ying the control.

For dessert, Gerry dressed in various outfits before he crept over: thief, soldier, cop, even once he was a most convincing construction worker who hooted and hollered at Ying until she made him pay.

Ying dressed always in her precious white leather outfit, which was becoming more supple with wear, like Gerry. Ying found new ways to punish him: a cat of nine tails, a thick leather belt, a willow switch, clamps, a nasty long purple dildo she dubbed "the enforcer." Gerry took everything she could deliver.

Mornings after were tender. Sometimes they made love; sometimes they sat cross-legged, nude on the bed, sipped tea and talked. They talked of childhood, of fears and frustrations, joys and jubilations. She even told him about G.I. Joe. The day he mounted a hook like the one in his bedroom on Ying's ceiling, Gerry told that he was a young executive, very powerful, and struggled with the stresses of his job. "I'm a control freak, Ying." "Doesn't show," she replied. He simply smiled at her. But the way he seemed to shrug her off when she said she truly understood his stresses was one of the rare things about him she did not like. As a matter of fact, the session after that, she tied him down face first and reamed him with "the enforcer" until he came on her satin sheets. She stood on his ass and made him lick up the mess.

He was a bottomless pit for punishment, and she became envious. She remembered how she felt as she took part in Red's punishment. An urge grew like the need for sexual release after a month of complete abstention. This urge didn't abate even when Gerry gave her seven strong orgasms on his knees, his hands bound behind his back, head tilted back so far that he had trouble straightening it up when she was done.

She wondered who was master and who was slave.

As she prepared for the next mealtime trappings, she recalled there was only one time where he seemed to have truly been beaten: ironically, the first time the thief had come.

She wondered if the true wall to dominance was a form of submission.

She delved into copious research.

It was clear in Gerry's expression that he detected a change as she forced him to strip his thief outfit but did not punish him. She cuffed him and pulled him into the bedroom. A small table sat near the dangling hook with a burner and a jar warming on it. He looked down at his nude body with eyes wide. She pushed him toward the hook. "I own you."

She had raised the hook and had to help him put his cuffed hands in it with the aid of a chair. He could barely keep steady.

She stirred the goop in the jar.

His eyes were like that first night. He remained so very still.

Ying started on his back, applying the warm goop to a small stretch. He had little hair back there, but grunted as she pressed on the muslin strips and yanked them methodically away.

After his back, she goosed his jaw like a snapdragon. Taking a kiss from her had become the symbol of his "surrender." Despite the anger in his eyes, his mouth gaped for a kiss.

He didn't yell out, the way he did when she whipped him, as she stripped his legs. She stroked his jaw and his mouth opened even more slowly. She kissed him even deeper, and then stood on the chair to strip his arms.

The anger had drained from his eyes. She wondered if she had gone too far. But he'd told her about "safe words" on their second outing. She traced his jaw and watched his mouth slowly open. He didn't say the word. She stirred the wax and looked at his furry chest. He closed his eyes and accepted her tongue. She lingered on the kiss like a long goodbye.

His cock pointed at the ceiling as she fixed the first strip to him. His grunts were now just an explosion like a massive compressor releasing all its air. He yanked so hard she was sure she heard the studs above him groan. She stripped every last bit of chest hair, and then finally looked at his crotch. He shook his head. She nodded. She stroked his cock, and then laced her fingers in the last frontier of his body hair.

"Now you are truly mine." It was the first time she'd deliberately eschewed her Chinese accent during the punishments.

He compressed his jaw. She stroked it, and it slowly opened. She applied the muslin above his cock. She gave him a deep, long kiss during which she ripped the last furry strips away. He was limp, quiet, resolved as this last vestige was removed. She curled her fingers around his furry scrotum and smiled. His eyes shocked wide, but he nodded, and then opened his mouth. She shook her head and let go of his testicles. She helped him from the hook and led him to the shower. He braced to her and moved slowly. She methodically cleaned his smooth pink body with cool water and floral soap. His cock lifted toward the showerhead, and she took it deep in her mouth. Fellatio was another thing Gerry had refused to accept from her. Ying applied every trick she knew, and some she conjured on the spot. She nibbled the base, tongued his balls, and then settled on the head with a few deft twirls of her tongue. He writhed harder and harder, almost as if trying to escape, but he shot into the back of her throat. He had to grab her head to remain upright as he squirted ribbon after ribbon into her gullet.

She drank him, steadied him, dried his body and led him to bed.

Another first, he fell asleep before Ying. She cupped his back and ran her fingers through the long golden hair on his head. His silky skin felt bizarre.

The next morning, Ying awoke to feel Gerry's big hands stroking every inch of her; it felt possessive. He eased her onto her back, pulled her knees to her chest, and compressed her. His big smooth arms surrounded her knees and folded arms.

He pushed into her sharply, before she was wet and the friction was heaven. The way he bumped her cervix wasn't, but she resisted even the slightest hint of a grimace. She smiled softly. He gripped the V of her pubic hair, squeezed her breasts a little extra tight, bit the nape of her neck. She flowed and her depths opened as he pumped her.

She went limp and bounced with his weight. She realized what he was giving her was just a fraction of his power, and it felt so very perfect.

She closed her eyes and dared to dream that he understood now.

The next night of mealtime trappings, Gerry's room remained dark. Ying checked the clock. 8:05. She sighed, sat down, and took the first bite of her meal. She began to worry if indeed he did understand. She wondered if her taking him to total submission, and then servicing him, had broken some spell. She wondered if the powerful fuck the morning after and the sweet, long kiss at the door after breakfast was his goodbye.

It seemed forever until his light came on. Her stomach turned as she looked down at her new outfit again. She worried so much that she covered her chest in a display of modesty that seemed to be rare these days.

She felt dizzy for lack of air. When he appeared, Ying gasped. Her hands drained to her sides.

Jeremy was clad, shoulder to shank, in gleaming jet-black leather, a riding crop in his hand. He turned to the long neglected hook in his room and pushed it so it swung like Poe's pendulum. Ying tugged the neck of her skin-tight black shirt, and then grazed her hard nipples. Her pussy flowed like the Yangtze.

Ying looked side to side, as if trying to evade detection. Gerry briefly smiled, and then nodded. The two meals sat on their tables, destined to fall cold. The leather over Gerry's groin could barely contain the bulge.

She hesitated at the corner of her apartment building, with a view of his windows as the last light was extinguished. Chills stroked her spine like fingers. She wondered how much it would take to make her truly surrender.

She trusted Gerry would be as diligent in his search as was her vow to resist.

Dreams from a Black Chrysalis

By
Jason Rubis

It moved a very little, and was breathing. When it opened its eyes Molly squeaked and jumped back, hissing, "Shit, *shit!*" But the eyes at least proved that it was a human being and not—as Molly had initially thought—some bizarre piece of sculpture Hachi had tucked away in her closet. It didn't seem to be in any particular discomfort, but the breathing—a slow and steady rasping through its nostrils—seemed somehow plaintive.

"Are you okay? Hello?" Molly approached the closet door with some reluctance, as though afraid the bundle of person in there might suddenly lash out science fiction tentacles to seize her ankles. Molly used to love horror movies. She knew exactly how she would dig her nails into the carpet, shrieking as she was dragged into the closet, the door slamming shut on her with great finality. Later Hachi would go in the closet for something and find her bones.

The person didn't answer or make any sign that it had heard her. The reason Molly could gather nothing of its gender or age was that it was encased in a costume of black latex. It was the sort of costume that extended—not unlike children's pajamas—into gloves at the wrists and thick-soled boots at the ankles. A mask covered its head, with holes at the nostrils to allow that disturbing breathing, and two more holes at the eyes. Molly couldn't see what color this person's eyes were—she was leery of getting *too* close—though she could see that they were large and dark and sad.

The person was crouched on a row of shoes on the floor of Hachi's closet, in what had to be a fantastically uncomfortable position: head down, ass up. Its wrists were bound at the small of its back with what appeared to be black rubber tubing. More tubing—and strips of black cloth—secured its ankles. It appeared to be trying to make itself as compact and as immobile as possible. Various outfits of Hachi's—suits, raincoats, negligee—swung just above it, brilliant colors in stark contrast with the latex.

"Did Hachi...this is something you were doing with Hachi, right? Do you want me to untie you, or...?" Again, no answer but that creepy breathing. Molly retreated slowly, gnawing her thumb. Eventually she ran downstairs and fixed herself a large glass of iced vodka.

The situation was extremely uncomfortable. There was, of course, nothing preventing her from simply calling Hachi in London and demanding to know who this strange person in the closet was. It would have been extremely satisfying at that moment to inform Hachi—with suitable indignation, needless to say—that house-sitting, undertaken as a favor to a friend, did not normally include babysitting said friend's sex-slaves.

The problem was that Molly had found Latex (as she found herself thinking of the bound person) while snooping in Hachi's bedroom. There was no other way to put it. Though she loved to brag about her "friendship" with Hachiko Ozu, Molly was all too aware that the designer regarded her less as a friend than an amusing kind of puppy, to be petted and laughed at or ignored as the situation demanded. They had met at a club through mutual acquaintances (considerably higher-placed socially than Molly) and most of their encounters since had been at other clubs, totally at random, though Hachi did generally reply—dependably if rather dryly—to Molly's emails.

Hachi was an androgynous Eurasian beauty, as well-known in the SM demimonde as she was in the fashion world. Hachi had a career and several houses in different cities in different countries. Molly was a twenty-three-year-old club-rat with a loft, a trust fund, and little else to recommend her beyond a certain bratty cuteness.

So when the chance to house-sit for Hachi had emerged, she'd jumped at it, figuring it would give her a nearly endless fund of bragging-currency. And the moment she knew Hachi's plane was off the ground, Molly had begun a methodical exploration of her house, beginning in the kitchen. So far it had been incredibly disappointing. There had been no secret caches of bizarre/possibly illegal pornography, no diaries detailing orgies with the rich and famous, and no drugs beyond the overflowing liquor cabinet and half a pack of Gauloises she had found in one of the guest bathrooms. There was Hachi's basement dungeon, of course, but everyone knew about *that*.

By the time she had gotten to the bedroom, Molly had resigned herself to rifling through Hachi's wardrobe. That, at least, was sure to be kind of fabulous. Instead, she had found Latex.

It had been agreed that Molly would sleep in a small but comfortable room on the first floor. On entering the house, Molly had found Hachi's own bedroom door pointedly closed, though not actually locked. Molly was not sure what would happen if she phoned her about Latex. She had never seen the designer angry. On the other hand, she had witnessed her sarcasm, many times. She felt little interest in being on the receiving end again.

Down in the kitchen, Molly lit a cigarette to help her vodka down, and gave some thought to next steps. Obviously Latex was there of his (after several sips, she had decided the person in the closet was male) own free will. In the unlikely event he were some kind of prisoner, he would certainly have taken the opportunity to kick up a fuss when Molly opened the closet door. She had read about experiments in "sensory deprivation." Obviously this was one of them. It was exactly the kind of edgy play that Hachi was famous for.

More troublesome was the fact that even if Molly simply ignored Latex for the rest of her stay, she had no idea what Hachi would hear from him upon her return. Perhaps he would be discreet about the house-sitter's indiscretion. On the other hand, perhaps he would be angry. Perhaps he would be furious. Molly had visions of a furious Latex, cuddled in the arms of an equally indignant Hachi, delivering a hissing diatribe against the little bitch who had disturbed his "meditation."

Hachi had left her kitchen well-stocked and told Molly to help herself to anything she liked. She had also left instructions at a local, very good French restaurant that the young lady staying at Miss Ozu's house should be sent over anything she cared to call and ask for, on Miss Ozu's tab. But Molly was not especially hungry, and after she finished draining her glass she was still less inclined to eat. Instead, she poured another and put on a CD of club mixes that had been burned for Hachi by a rather notorious Manhattan DJ, a man rumored to be insanely in love with her feet.

As Molly danced with herself, improvising clumsy steps she would never have had the nerve to try in the clubs, she found herself thinking of Latex. Of his strange sad eyes. The more she thought, the more certain she became that Hachi's slave (or whatever he was) bore her no ill will. In fact, she began feeling that, in that odd moment when she had looked into his eyes, they had on some level bonded. She was aware that there wasn't much more to this feeling than to her pretense that she and Hachi were friends, but it persisted. It was, certainly, a very appealing feeling.

The conviction grew in her that she needed to check on Latex, that perhaps he was regretting passing up the opportunity to be freed. Imagining herself in Latex's place even for a moment made Molly squirmingly uncomfortable. She feared pain of any kind, though images of suffering were attractive to her. The thought of Latex lying crouched and twisted on a lumpy, pungent bed of Hachi's old shoes fascinated and appalled her. It also made her run a hand over her breast, stiffening the nipple in a quick, perfunctory caress, and pulling away, as though she was afraid of being caught.

She went to her room and, on an obscure impulse, changed into a short black dress she had for no good reason brought along. By now she had passed beyond a comfortable tipsiness into true inebriation. When she made up her face, her hand was unsteady, as were her steps when she began making her way back to Hachi's room. She was aware that she had not put panties on under her little dress, but was not entirely sure if the omission had been deliberate.

The warm excitement she had felt was now tinged with apprehension, almost fear. She felt like she was going to a lover, but a lover who might turn out to be a ghost or a monster. She had, after all, no real idea what Latex was really like. Horrible possibilities occurred to her, and then wonderful ones. All of this gradually turned her feelings more and more towards the erotic. When she stepped into Hachi's room and heard the ragged hiss of Latex's breathing, it made a little jolt of arousal in her belly.

"Hey," she said. "It's me, I'm back. Are you okay?" By now she knew better than to expect an answer. She stepped lightly towards the open door of the closet. The room was now dark but she felt oddly disinclined to turn on a light.

"I'm sorry if I'm disturbing you or anything. Am I? If you want me to go...?" It surprised her a little how coy her voice sounded. She slid down to her knees and touched Latex's cheek—gingerly at first. Then, uncurling her fingers, she laid her whole palm on the top of his head. The black rubber felt warm—not really feverish, more as though Latex were some life-form whose body temperature was naturally higher than that of humans.

When he made no response, Molly began running her palms over his back and legs. She did this mindlessly, enjoying the smooth feel of the rubber. The suit was nearly skin-tight and smelled pungently, like nothing human. Hesitating a moment, Molly leaned forward and pressed her lips against his shoulder in a silent kiss. She opened her mouth and bit gently. Briefly she imagined herself eating Latex like a giant black jujube, taking greedy bites that left nothing but smoothly scalloped indentations in his onyx flesh. She licked the spot she had bitten, and then kissed the slick place her saliva had made.

Soon she was curling over Latex in a fervent embrace, stroking and kneading shamelessly, kissing and mouthing the irregularities and protrusions of his/her body. In a very little time she had thrown a leg over him and was—there could be no other word for it—humping him. Rubbing her bare, now very wet, pussy first against a spot on his ass, and then—once a small but very satisfactory orgasm had been reached—moving greedily over to the smooth bunch of his fingers.

What Latex thought of this Molly couldn't imagine, and preferred not to try. She was lost in a hazy, very pleasurable rush of tenderness mingled with desire. More, she felt *permitted* to do this, that somehow it was *alright* for her to take advantage of Latex's body in this way. It was not unlike, in an odd way, the first time she had been fucked.

This feeling was vindicated when the rubbery fingers curled themselves around her crotch. A little of the horror-movie feeling came back and Molly almost tumbled off; then Latex's fingers, clumsily at first, but with a certain knowing efficiency, began playing with her pussy. Molly was breathlessly delighted at this, the first time that Latex actually responded to her in any meaningful way.

The second orgasm made her sleepy. She curled herself up next to Latex, holding him with both arms and pillowing her head on his shoulder. In moments, whispering little endearments, she fell asleep.

Her dream was strange. She was in a kind of high-tech, *Blade Runner*-esque fetish nightclub, the kind she had always imagined that certain Asian cities—Tokyo, say—were rife with. There were people everywhere, dark people everywhere she looked, all dressed in intricate outfits of leather and plastic with breastplates of shining chrome. Molly had no idea what she herself was wearing. She might have been wearing a leather costume of her own, or she could as easily have been naked.

There was a definite sense of expectation in the air. The dark people were waiting for her to do something. At first she had no idea what this might be. Then she noticed the hanging person.

At first the shape seemed very much like Latex, swaddled all over in strips of some kind of black material—rubber or PVC. More strips connected the shape's weight to the ceiling, like an umbilicus. At other moments the shape's covering changed, sprouting wide holes that revealed pale flesh—large-nippled breasts and a plump bulge of shaved, very wet pussy peeking between the thighs. It was very evidently a woman, hanging in a fetal position, its knees drawn up to its chest.

Molly became certain the woman was Hachi. Hachi's eyes were shut, her mouth hanging open in a way that suggested both sexual ecstasy and brain damage. Molly stood looking up at her friend's slowly revolving form. It was unnerving seeing Hachi in such a helpless position—even in a place like this, where imprisonment would surely be voluntary. Hachi wasn't like that. Molly found herself sobbing.

The dark people in the club seemed to share her misery. Molly was hugged and kissed and caressed, in what she took to be a ritual of preparation. Then she was clinging to Hachi, a massive knife in her hand. She had no idea who had given her the knife or how she had gotten up to Hachi. She had the vague notion that she had somehow risen on her own power; she imagined a graceful, slow-motion leap.

Music was now playing, something harsh and techno. Molly sawed with the curved blade at the fleshy black strips that held Hachi to the ceiling. As she did this, she kissed her friend's face—however clumsily, this was something she had always wanted to do. The fact that she was kissing Hachi seemed enormous, momentous, and filled her with a tearful pride. She whispered, "It's okay, baby. Okay? It's all good. I love you, okay? You're alright."

Then the strips parted, and she and Hachi fell an enormous distance, plummeting together to the floor.

Latex's moan woke her. Molly jerked awake, crying out with a dry mouth. She was not immediately sure where she was, only that she was in a little cramped space, lying on top of something warm and smooth and somewhat human-shaped. There was sunlight through the windows, but it was from a dim, just-risen sun.

Latex moaned again—loudly and emphatically, and twitched. There was no doubt he was in pain—or at least severe discomfort. He wanted out of his rubber suit, there wasn't much doubt of that either.

"Oh my God." Molly staggered to her feet, finding a moment to agonize over how badly wrinkled her little dress had gotten. "Are you okay?"

"Mmmmnnnnnnggghhh…"

"Oh shit, oh shit. Okay, okay, hold on…"

Molly couldn't seem to walk or think properly. Her first impulse was to run out of the house screaming for help, but Latex's moaning had her convinced that he was in terrible pain, that every minute wasted cost him agonies.

Untie him. She had to untie him first. She fell to her knees and began plucking hopelessly at the rubber tubing at his wrists. It was no good; the knots were from hell, as big as her thumbs.

Knife. Something sharp. Molly scrambled out of the bedroom, making for the stairs. There were knives in a wooden block on the kitchen counter, their image glowed in her mind like the grail, but she had to hurry. Latex was moaning furiously now, shaking all over. Halfway down the stairs Molly could hear him thrusting himself around in the closet.

At the foot of the stairs, she remembered the knives on Hachi's living room wall. There was a large selection of them, hung in display along with antique swords and shields. Molly snatched at one, and then nearly screamed in frustration; the hilt was wired securely to the wall.

The kitchen, then. But it was too far away, and Latex was still crying. Molly picked up a heavy ashtray and bludgeoned the knife from the side. The pegs it was wired to gave way with a satisfying rain of dust and broken plaster, and a moment later she was running back to Hachi's room, dagger in hand. Unlike the knife in her dream, it was straight, double-edged. But she had no doubt it would do the job, and it did; applied to the knots holding Latex's wrists, they parted like butter.

Latex's hands fell to his sides and twisted feebly on the floor. He had stopped moaning, but was breathing explosively in and out of the mask-holes. Molly cut the tubing at his ankles and pushed him, one-handed, onto his side, and then rolled him onto his back.

As carefully as she could, she pierced the rubber with the dagger's point, keeping the blade flat against Latex's side. He shook his head and fumbled at her shoulder, puffing through the mask. But Molly was convinced the suit had to come off. He was suffocating or something. Hadn't she heard somewhere that you had to be careful with these rubber bondage-suits, that they didn't let the skin breathe, or something?

"It's okay, she'll understand. I'll buy you a new one, Jesus Christ." Worried as she was about Latex, she found it deeply satisfying to curl her fingers into the gap she had made in the rubber and pull. It parted silently, revealing a flat belly, its darkish-complected skin gleaming with sweat.

Another tug showed that Latex had small but firm breasts, with tiny, erect nipples. He wasn't a he at all.

Molly didn't have time to be astonished. By now Latex had given up struggling and had joined her in peeling away the remains of the suit. She loosened something at the nape of her neck and laboriously tugged the mask off.

Latex was small and thin, with large teeth and very short dark hair and the same large, beautiful eyes Molly remembered. "Christ," she breathed, in an unidentifiable accent. "Christ, Hachi's going to kill me."

"No, it's okay." Molly found it necessary to say this. She felt terribly angry at Hachi. She put her arms around the small woman, who a moment later, a little uncertainly, returned the embrace.

Latex's body stank of sweat and rubber, but Molly couldn't stop herself from kissing it, moving her lips up to those tiny nipples. Latex murmured and slid her nails over Molly's shoulders.

"I got a cramp," she explained. "Hurt like fuck. I should have known it would happen." She was short of breath, but sounded perfectly reasonable, as though she were not, in fact, having her nipples sucked. "Hachi tried to warn me, actually. I wanted to go through with it, like an idiot. God, she'll laugh at me."

The phone began ringing suddenly, a strident, harsh sound that made Molly start. She ground her teeth when it didn't stop.

"That'll be Hachi. Babe, let me go?"

Latex tried to pull away and get the phone, but Molly wouldn't let her; she held her tightly, pressed her closed eyes against the bony chest. If she struggled, Molly intended to push backward with all her strength, bite her if necessary. She had been through too much. She wasn't going to let her go now. There were limits.

Blade, Ink, Steel

By
Sharon Wachsler

To the Skin

Too early, no sleep, on Ella's arm, all's black. Buzzed on java shots, skittering heels stick in cracked linoleum, I stumble, catch a wheezing laugh far left. Ella shoves me onto a chair, quick unlocks one cuff, yanks my wrist to the armrest. *Click, click, click* it closes, and swift she does the other. Seat clanks up like a dentist chair. Ankle shackles ratcheted to a bar below.

Ella jerks off my blindfold. In sudden flickering fluorescence, dented metal mirror exposes my waxy skin, red-lined eyes. Ella drops into a rocker, nods to coughing tough crushing out her cig in the dim. Tar-fingered stranger slouches over, scissors in one hand, clippers in the other, fists the chestnut hank hanging from my nape to ass. "Nuh!" I toss my head, sick rises at the *snick, snick, snick* of quick blades.

"Good we've got that ball gag in, eh, Sweet Pea?" Ella smirks. "I'd be so disappointed if you didn't appreciate Gen's work."

Sweet Pea. I purple: gentle, dainty taunt. If I could spit it, those words – not my hair – would be on the floor, ground into the grimy vinyl.

Gen bows me. Clippers devour vanity in jagged arcs, tears canyon between cheeks and nose. Then she sits to watch.

Ella stalks up, jacks my skirt to my hips, lifts Gen's shears, with a flick she fillets my panties, tosses the scissors and pries me apart. Scooping my severed braid from the floor, she fans it up my thighs, tickling it against my pulsing cunt, bristles sharp and soft – too light. I jut toward the tease.

Laughter. "What, no tears now?" Ella feeds the dark shock inside me, brown ponytail swirling my cunt, silken ends whisper at pussy lips. I strain at the restraints, loose a whimper. She snakes it out, glistening with creme, smears my cheeks, chin, nose with my reek. Lazing, she puts the twist between her teeth, sucking like a cigar. Nods to Gen, "Tastes like a cunt."

Then Gen's back, cutting relentless. Wielding a razor, scrapes my scalp.

The scratching distracts me as Ella throws my damp hank in my lap, releases a wrist. "Unbraid it," she says. Shaking, my fingers finish, she reclasps the wrist.

She licks her lips to suck the end again, flicks her Zippo, flames the tip. Brunette spider's threads curl quick like spent filament. She drops it in a chipped glass dish as it opens into charred gray dust.

I sit transfixed till Gen spins me, holding a second mirror behind. The front's still a blunt cut, but from nape to crown the back's a quarter-inch except the stark letters carved to the skin, not even stubble there: *E L L A ' S*. I quiver as Ella uncuffs me to run my hands over her name. Over and over and over. ELLA'S. Over and over.

Flipping Gen ten bills, Ella grins, "Get lost for twenty." Pumps the chair low, unzips her jeans to unleash her dick, my mouth. I reach, one hand finds her cock, the other fingers my scalp, and suck her: heaven. Now I know, Samson should've kissed Delilah's dick.

Tight and hot I blow till her stained fingers push mine away. She rakes me with blunt nails and I feel her brand – the razor burn.

In the Skin

Ella recuffs and gags me, frees my feet, flags a cab, herds me onto vinyl. Dizzy with possession, I rock, thighs squeezed, rubbing my scalp against the seat, reading it like inverted Braille. Vise-grips my wrist, she snarls low so the driver's not wise, "Trying to get off?" Slicks two fingers under my skirt and into me. I gasp, arch to get her deeper.

Slap, slap, she smacks the Plexi. "Next Seven-Eleven."

Cab swings wide, and Ella jerks out of me and cab. My yelp muffled, I shiver in the empty. Back, she cradles cherry soda and yogurt, releases my mouth, strawing the drink. "Suck like it's mine," she squeezes her crotch. I gulp the sweet while she tumbles the yogurt. "How would you eat yourself?" I lap the spoon.

Low, "You're too in your head. I'm getting into your body." I moan. "Know why it's all cherry? Cuz I'm gonna bust yours all day, Sweet Pea."

The dairy sours. I choke it down, open for the gag. "Good." Then, "Here!" She hollers. Cabbie jams to the side, Ella's pulling me out before I read the signs. Inside, walls crawl with arms, backs, necks, lined, linked, inked. I skitter back, but Ella's palming my skull. "What do you say?" She rubs: *ELLA'S*.

"Tina!" She belts.

A juicy olive femme dances in, hands her a drawing. "Beauty, eh?"

Ella pats her ass. "Perfect."

Tina swings to her table. "Hop up!" she caresses it. Ella hoists me.

Tina smiles, lays paper in my lap, talking as she traces a lithe stem branching up, delicate fronds unfurling. "These two little blossoms will be white," the tattooist points a red-tipped finger. "The leaves, stem, and pod will all be green of course. Sweet, eh?"

They turn to me. I freeze. All I see: that tender vine.

"So," Tina lays down her pen. "Read and sign this – consent, liability, notice of safety practices, etcetera." I see the exit, my chance.

Ella rises, steps toward it.

I scribble, fitful, my signature illegible. Ella pivots, flashes "lay down." Casual, she flicks my skirt back, baring me. "It will fit?"

Crimson, I cringe. Tina frowns, "Don't you want this?" Motions to my mouth. "Better take that out."

I look down, try to catch Ella's eye, but she's turned, tracing her name in caps on a scrap, a big apostrophe "S," gaze lazing to the door.

Tina touches my face with a lacquered nail. "Hon, you're the one who'll wear it. You gotta love it." I swallow the lump, nod, let myself fall limp as Ella walks over again.

Tina unwraps gel and razors. "Great," beaming. "The stem'll start here," a red-tipped finger touches above my thigh, "avoid the crease, leaves and flowers curling up . . ." Finger arcs my mound. "A pod hanging on each *labia majora.*"

Ella sits to the side, I press my head into the table to feel the empty places, tasting pools of magic cherry Kool-Aid in my mind. Watch her watching Tina shave me smooth, transfer the pattern. I slip into the *slick, slick, slick* and Ella's eyes.

Then a million burning needles break my skin. The stabbing switches on and off with soothing swipes. Lidocaine cream, I learn later, makes it such a pure pain, tides of cool and hot rocking me. A minute, ten, a hundred, endless – wipe, burn, wipe, burn, holding still, exposed, exquisite. The searing juices my cunt, heat rising pungent past Tina's needles.

Four hours gone: I'm drunk on pain, Ella's triumph, Tina's rhythmic *swipe, sting, swipe, sting,* as she wipes away black and green and white – and red so beautiful, can't believe I'm setting it free.

I'm desperate for Ella's dick, tongue, thumb, touch. Finally, Tina flashes glass at me. In the mirror, I'm transformed: Ella's tender cunt.

Through the Skin

Aftercare words blur as Ella pays, pushes me into to a back room chair, sits on its counter. Blissed, I eye Ella's dick, try to tickle my clit. Slaps my hand – "Lucille!" she bellows.

Billy-Idol dyke ambles in, gleaming metal beads.

Another paper. I sigh, sign, smiling. Unbutton my top, finger a nipple.

"She tweaking?" Cille frowns.

"Nah – endorphins. New tat," Ella lifts my skirt. I squirm forward, giving blondy a good look. She chuckles.

"You'll oversee aftercare?"

"What do you think?" Ella jaws.

"A'ight," Cille raises palms in surrender. "But take *that* out."

Ella scowls, releases my mouth. "Lean back, Sweat Pea," *sotto voce.* Ceiling swirls. She motions to Cille.

"Here," Ella touches my uninked, inside labia.

"Oh," I tilt toward it.

"And here."

"Aye-ah," I wriggle.

Lucille shakes her head, looking down at me. "I can't do this if you don't hold still."

"Ella touched me," I explain.

"Christ." Lucille slops coffee on her T.

Ella looms. "I'm chaining you. Don't move."

I nod, peaceful.

Astringent tingles my clit hood. Fantastic lights dance, but I statue. Purple pen dots, Ella and Cille eyeball angles, tilt, peer.

Then red-hot pinwheels fire left, clean pain – just a taste – the pulling, fishing-line fine, until the tug, when I think I might come, but it's not enough. Again the pierce, this time right, I bite back my cry. Sweet hurt, tickle, tug. Tightening, fastening clasps, that pinching has my hands gripping, Ella's tongue circles her lip.

Hand glass held below my open lap. "Here." Two tiny steel hoops, each gold-beaded, gold links hanging between. My pearl, pulsing pink, draped in gold.

Ella stealths to me, slipping her littlest finger under, tugs feathery. My eyes roll.

From her pocket Ella spins a new ring: thick gold band, a long strand dangles a clasp. "You'll heal, then who owns you, Sweet Pea?"

I make my mouth an "O." Ella slips the ring between my lips. Kingly, she holds her hand out to be kissed. I slide the ring down her fourth finger like unrolling a rubber, tasting the metal tang, licking her underside's wrinkles.

We kiss. Ella takes me home.

Shaping Genevieve

By
Theda Hudson

The head had been worked over really good. The face was curiously flat, making her look completely out of place for 400 BCE Greece. She was probably closer to 500 BCE by the way her hair had been redone into a thickly coiled halo. It was not unheard of; statues broke and people, then and now, reworked them.

Turning, I saw Genevieve on the chaise. She'd been worked over pretty good too. A livid bruise spread over her cheekbone and up across her eye. She was still wearing emerald, her favorite color, and eighteen months went *poof!* just like that. She met my gaze coolly, not a twitch saying she knew me. I could tell by the tightness around her eyes, the color in her cheeks. Oh, yes, *poof*.

My heart lurched, remembering what a delicate and subtle beauty Genevieve was. I looked to Victor Sadarno, the swarthy man I'd come to see about the head. He was in his early forties, overweight, and, I suspected, just a petty thief riding Lady Luck, completely ignorant of what he had.

"Here, Dalton." Victor handed the marble to me. A client, Timothy Blake, was interested in buying the heads. I was here to authenticate them. It was grayish interspersed with flecks of pure white light. Her nose had probably been broken and some artisan had shaved off layers until that grace and lightness was flattened, coarsened.

I changed position, seeking better light and glanced discretely at Genevieve. She had a tattoo ringing her left middle finger. *Essex Club* was one direction I'd never searched. And there she'd been, property. She wouldn't meet my eyes.

I looked back to Victor and handed him the sculpture. "She's quite a piece."

"You like her? I'll show you some others." I followed him to the study where six other heads sat on pedestals. They were all from Cyprus and the western Italian coast, dating about 500 BCE. That fit.

"Yes, yes, this is all quite good, excellent." I smiled affably.

"I have others."

"How many?"

"Twenty."

"Good, good." That fit too. I smiled again, and then paused. "Why'd you pick that one?"

"I just picked one up. Why, is it special?"

I thought of that flattened face, that thick halo, Genevieve on the couch.

"Yes, yes, she's special," to have suffered at such inept, ignorant hands, I finished to myself. This would be a pleasure.

Victor smiled. "Then you'll tell Mr. Blake?"

"Yes."

Victor, pleased at the good day's work he'd done, was magnanimous.

"Would you like a glass of wine?"

"Yes, thanks."

We drank companionably for a few moments.

"I noticed the woman's ring," I said, showing I knew the rules.

"Yes," he said with pride. "Her name is Genevieve. Do you want to use her?"

Use her. "It would be a nice perk. But I must rely on your generosity for toys."

Letting me use her lent him a certain amount of cachet and gave us other connections. "Of course. I haven't got many toys myself, though."

I shrugged; he preferred a blunter approach.

"Go back in," he said. "I'll bring my case."

"Thank you very much, Victor."

I paused in the entry to the living room. Genevieve was posed on the chaise lounge facing me. I could see lines on her face, around those precious lips, so soft and yielding when she became my bottom three years ago.

How much was it worth to try again? Was there enough left to refashion, like that marble head? Did she even want me to try, knowing the unyielding price?

"Answer yes or no," I said as I went to her. "Do you understand?" It came out harsher than I'd intended.

"Yes," she whispered, dropping her eyes.

"This is not about that tattoo on your finger, *this* is about you and me and the scene we have yet to finish." I swore I was boring holes straight into her. I wanted to be.

"Yes," she said, clearly remembering that unfinished moment eighteen months ago.

"Then do exactly as you are told," I continued. "Do you understand?" *Do you trust me?*

"Yes." She still didn't look at me and I let it go for now. Either she would act or it would be over, and I would do whatever it took to be numb again.

"What do you want, Genevieve?"

Tears were bright in her eyes. Swallowing tightly, she said, "To completely and abjectly offer myself to whatever you'll have of me."

I growled. It was not enough; such a shapeless and unformed offer had no appeal for me.

"Insufficient, but I accept it *for this moment*. Do you understand?"

"Yes. Thank you."

I could barely hear her.

Victor came back. "Well, here you are."

He handed me a black leather case, barely as long as the crop and the short canes. Not a lot but was all quality work. I pulled out two floggers, a paddle, and a decent set of cuffs. Not fur lined. I looked to her again.

Poor thing. She'd so loved her fur. It was typical of the Essex Club. Everything was sensational and coarse, skimming the power trip, missing the sacred place of the white light where people like Genevieve danced.

I hefted the black leather cuffs and winked at Victor.

Victor laughed. "May I watch?"

I bowed. "By all means."

Victor took a seat in the easy chair to the side.

I motioned and Genevieve stood. Her hand was cold as I led her to the fireplace. The embers were warm.

"Let us begin. Show me what you have." She looked down as the emerald green caftan slipped off. Her body was milk white, marred now by more than three moles and my cutting. There were several old scars and burns. She was pierced too on her cunt lips and left nipple. I wasn't sure if I was more angry at the abuse or pleased to find a little seasoning.

I gestured her to turn. Her waist still rode the rising swell of her hips. That last night I had lined up the paddle on her ass and she had whimpered. The moment the paddle lifted she moaned, turning it into a great cry when it landed on her red flesh. She liked me to make her count. She would forget so I kept starting over.

I was angry with her for bringing me to this. I lifted a cuff. She proffered her hand and I placed the leather around her wrist. There was a scar there now, bad rub.

I had searched where I could, pulled in what favors I had. Nothing. I let it lie then, figuring she hadn't *wanted* to be found. But there was always that question, did I do enough? And now knowing where she'd been ... I was the first to drop my eyes.

I gestured roughly with the other cuff and she obliged with a triumphant tilt of her head because I had looked away first. I buckled the cuff and snapped the two together with a decisive click. I shook them a little and looked to her, smiling. *Yes? Is it like that?*

I snapped the leash onto the other end of the clip, ran the leather through the carving on the mantle, and snapped it back to the other end. The cuffs weren't really necessary. It was all part of the symbolism, the trappings of the scene, rife with meaning, heavy with the weight of shared understanding.

I nudged her legs apart with my foot and allowed my coat to brush against her back. She shivered and I smiled. She loved wool.

"Keep your legs spread just like this," I said for Victor's benefit. "Say, 'Oh, sir,' if you become fatigued or require. Do you understand?"

"Yes, sir." Her voice was hoarse. This too was the same. I was angry when I turned to Victor. "May I have water?"

He got up. "Sure, sure." I'd reinforced his belief in the value of the sculptures and was now doing the same for his harlot. He poured a glass from the bar and placed it on the table.

I picked up both floggers. The deerhide was thirty or so half-inch wide falls for a total lashing power of about nothing, too soft for much more than a tactile toy. Genevieve'd always loved those toys. I could spank her crimson and she'd moan and offer her ass up for the heaviest blows I could muster as long as some softness stroked her periodically.

The moosehide flogger though, by her own admission, was like being hit by a two-by-four. Very thuddy, very good. I would warm her up with a thorough taste of it as a prelude for the paddle and the moment waiting for us. I slid the heavy flogger over her back, lightly flicking the thick fall of tails across her back, her thighs, her ass. When she began to sway, I hooked it around her neck. She groaned and I ran my hand down her side and stepped away.

She took the glass when I handed it to her. "I will flog you," I said. "You'll show me where you desire the strokes by how you offer yourself. Do you understand?"

"Yes," she replied, handing it back. Behind us, Victor grunted.

I lingered, letting her immerse herself in the ritual we were going to enact together. When the wind and the kinetic energy snicked out of the lashes next to her, she froze. The falls snapped in a fury around her, gauging weight and aim. I paused and rolled my neck on my shoulders. There was a series of pops and that tension rose up and out the top of my head.

The first stroke landed exactly across the center of those perfect apples. She hissed and I laughed. I followed up with a volley of light strokes designed to reacquaint us.

Dancing lightly on the balls of her feet, her hips swayed. My dick was rock hard and my feet remembered the rhythm of their dance. She offered her ass to me. When it dropped, I stepped in and stroked those smooth, hot cheeks, whispering, "Good little bottom, good, good Genevieve."

She moaned deeply, almost sobbing. I moved back, beginning to flog her in earnest with the deer hide. I chastised her back, flailed down her thighs, up the inside, and pressed the stock up between her legs. She moaned, riding it extravagantly.

She'd always been a fine slut. It made public play such a pleasure. I leaned in on her now. She pressed her tender ass against the wool of my pants. When I reached around, I discovered the glow of the fire had made the nipple ring warm. My hands remembered her beautiful, small, tight breasts and my fingers slid up to pinch the pegs of her nipples.

She groaned and her ass lifted up against my crotch. My dick pressed against her. I pinched harder and she whimpered, beginning to make the high, thin little cry that came with tit play.

When I allowed her to stand again, I lifted the moosehide and laid the deerhide in its place. The heft of it brought out a remembered rhythm. She would know this was the final preparation for the paddle and the moment we were building up to.

I gave her sets of five and seven and nine, stopping between to stroke her flesh or run my hand up into her sex and knead that hard knob. She was sopping, begging for release, the first of as many as the sly harlot could get from her bottomless jar.

I stood back to appreciate the even blush along her firm cheeks. I laid into them again along the midline. She danced, offering herself and accepting my touch, drinking in the heat, the sizzle between us. I could have swung all night.

She was not going to ask. She moaned when I finally laid the flogger across her shoulder. I picked up the glass. Her eyes were glazed and she was limp in the cuffs. She always said she never remembered to ask for water because her soul sipped the ambrosia I served up.

I made eye contact with Victor. He nodded, tipping his glass at me—a good show.

The paddle was oak, thin, and lightly varnished. I tested it against my palm. She heard and sucked wind. She'd be glad of the warm-up when I used it on her. It was not too heavy, stingier than the thuddy paddle that precipitated her flight from me a year and a half before. That one had been bigger, heavier. I'd promised her seven and by three I could tell she didn't like it. But she didn't offer a word and I'd stubbornly refused to ask, trying to force her to own her power.

This is where that refusal had brought her. A savage wave of anger washed over me.

I aimed her straight for it again tonight. She would act in the scene and none of the last year and a half would matter, or I could put the whole thing to rest at last. My breath was hot on her neck and the paddle was cool on her ass as it slid around and around.

"I'll give you nine blows with this paddle. If, at any time, you wish to stop, you'll say, 'Oh, sir.' Do you understand?"

I knew why she was with Victor. It wouldn't do any good to ask him to stop, to say to him, "I've had enough." So she was relieved of the necessity with no need to fret about it. But that's not a scene, that's a free-for-all and I wouldn't have it.

"Do you understand?" I growled in her ear. "Answer me, now."

"Yes, sir."

The paddling would play out here and now in front of Victor, who understood nothing. The fire popped loudly. I jerked.

"I understand, sir," she said snippily. Those little sparks always flared in her eyes when she saw my humanity, the crack in her view of the perfect top.

Or was it that she couldn't express those feelings herself and it was too much when others could?

"Very well, then. You will count. Carefully. No mistakes. Do you understand?"

"Yes, sir." Her tone signaled that she acknowledged the memory behind the question.

"Then we'll begin. Take the position." She bent over, proffering her ass.

The first hit was solid. A loud crack split the room. She sucked in breath and expelled it with an, "Owww," and then, belatedly, "One." It sounded sincere. Victor laughed. I stroked her ass gently and whispered in her ear, "Good Genevieve. Good, sweet bottom, no need to be brave now, dearest harlot, just be honest."

In answer she presented for the next stroke. Her hands clenched in the cuffs and the tendons stood out on the back of her thighs. She cried out at the next, which brought more laughter from Victor. "Two," she said tightly. I took a breath, held it, as I considered her now scarlet ass.

The third was a loud crack on the midline of her cheeks and she leaped forward. "Oh, three, ow, ow, ow," she sobbed. I stepped in and stroked her ass. It was hot and tight under my hand. The fire was warm on my face.

I gripped her arm tightly and spoke closely to her ear. "This is a scene, meant to be played, Genevieve, now enough of the theatrics, act."

Stepping to the other side, I laid the paddle on her ass. She moaned a little in anticipation and I lifted it, bringing it down solidly on the top of her cheeks. She would bear that mark for some time. "Oh, oh, four," she wailed and I thought she would do it then, prayed for her to say it. I covered her flesh with my pants, put an arm around her tightly as I reached across to pull on the steel ring in her nipple.

I drove my hips against her crimson ass and pinched her cunt lips together. She was still wet and her clit stood up under my fingers. She writhed under my touch and I let her bask in the knowledge of where I could take her. She was close to coming and I backed off to stroke her ass and remind her of where we were now.

She barely had time to get into position before I gave her the next. Victor clapped his hands, impressed. "Five," she said, sobbing.

I had never *asked* for it. I'd always insisted she be the one to *offer* it. Could that be the key? That I had to require her to act, instead of expecting her to act on her own?

I stepped back, swinging the paddle sharply behind her. The air whished and she sucked breath. I stepped in tight to her, coat rubbing roughly against her skin. "Yes, little slut, little bottom, this is what it does," I whispered in her ear, my fingers tight on that nipple ring. "Genevieve," I whispered urgently. "Meet me. *Own your power*. I require it."

We were frozen for a moment and I ran the paddle over that bruised flesh, the testament to our struggle. She groaned and offered herself to that gentle touch, dancing a little to tell me that she wanted this, asked for it, laid herself open to it and, by extension, me. But it wasn't enough. It was only one side.

My anger lifted the paddle and brought it down with all the weight of lost time. "Six, oh six, oh," she cried and, "Oh six, oh, sir, six, oh, sir, oh, sir," she kept repeating as if once said she could not stop.

She'd acted and the bottomless void acquired edges and limits and I could know her, now, truly and in depth.

I held her from behind, my cock driving against the hot, tender flesh of her ass. I took that nipple ring in my left hand and her clit in the other and brought her off in a gush that flowed over my hands and onto the carpet. She kept coming— all the months, the anguish, releasing, cleansing themselves in the hot flood of victory. I unhooked the leash and picked her up, made the few steps to the couch. The afghan that lay on the back enfolded her smoothly. I handed her the water.

She sipped gratefully, her eyes never leaving my face as I undid the cuffs and laid them aside. I took the glass back and only then did she relax. I stood, dried my hands on the towel Victor offered me, and finished my wine.

I let him lead me toward the door.

"I've never seen her like that; even at the club." He clapped me on the shoulder, caught between amazement and jealousy.

"Well, Victor, I'd like to thank you. It's been a very pleasurable evening."

"No, thank you. And if you know anybody else that might want those heads."

"Sure." I shook his hand and nodded to Genevieve, now staring at me over the back of the couch.

"Thank you." I left, got to my car, and flipped open my phone. "Cleebourn," I said, sitting back until he picked up.

"Dalton," he said, "why're you calling? Is there a problem?"

"No, no problem."

"Did he have them?"

"Yes, all twenty."

"I knew that shit stole them." Cleebourn paused. "So, again, why're you calling?"

"I want a favor."

"A favor? You're already well paid. Why should I do you a favor?"

"Because it's small and I'll give you a referral to make up for the inconvenience."

"Speak, I'm busy."

"There's a woman named Genevieve there. I want her treated good and taken out." Genevieve's old friend, Dame Vicky, would be happy to see her again until I had cleared my calendar.

"What's the referral?"

"I have a buyer. Guy named Blake. He's got money and a taste for antiquities that's not so refined it needs clean provenance."

There was a pause. Cleebourn knew I was good. That's why he retained me so often. It was no skin off his nose or his profit. "Okay. Anything else, Dalton?"

I paused, remembering that marble head with its flattened cheekbones and the livid bruise on Genevieve's face.

"Tell him I don't like his work."

There was silence. "Okay, I'll make sure he knows before they're finished with him. Go on, tell 'em whatever you want. I'm busy." I dialed another number. A man answered.

"It's me, Dalton. There's been a little change in plan."

I'd have time to gather the tools that delicate and subtle work demanded to fully smooth over the damage done. Then I'd explore Genevieve's new shape.

Down Below

By
Jean Roberta

"Do your students like Poe?" asked my department head, Dr. Dorothy Kipperwell. She generally discouraged modern informality in the English Department, but she had asked me to call her Kip. "Do they understand the language?"

"They do when I explain it to them," I told her. "A lot of first-year students are still teenagers, Kip. They understand extreme emotions. Adolescence is a gothic period. Remember how it felt to be that age?"

I knew that I was peeking through the keyhole of a locked door. Kip was almost butch enough to pass for a man (suave, witty, and middle-aged, but with plenty of controlled aggression) and she had told me enough about her life to let me know that her youth had been hell. The classic teenage whine that "nobody understands me" had been very true for her. Her lonely coming-of-age had made her tough, discreet, and determined to survive on her own terms. Beyond all reason, I wanted to be the one person on earth who could pierce her armor and learn her secrets.

Kip smiled in a way that raised the fine hair on the back of my neck. I hoped my nipples weren't poking up shamelessly under my low-cut red silk top, and I didn't dare look down.

Kip looked coolly professorial in a navy-blue sweater and pants. She also looked amused. "You like to revisit that period, don't you, Athena?"

I felt my face grow hot. I reminded myself that Kip wasn't much older than I was (thirty-something), or much taller. She was slim and muscular, but I was slim too. She had read a lot, of course, but that went with the territory; the same could be said about me. Like me, she had dark brown hair and eyes, although her eyes were smaller and looked more knowing than mine. Her hair looked short enough for the military, while mine flowed halfway down my back on occasions like this when it wasn't pinned up.

When we first met, Kip already knew that I had been a faculty brat all my life. She had heard of my parents: the historian Abraham Chalkdust and the linguist Anna Parle Chalkdust. If my pedigree impressed her, she didn't show it.

The quality in Kip that made me weak in the knees (even though I was not a weak person, as I reminded myself) seemed beyond my power to analyze. Telling myself that she was just an academic dyke like me didn't help me at all.

I ignored her last comment and plunged on with a discussion of my students, as though I were being interviewed for a job.

"They get the irony of the host's concern for his friend's health as the two men go deeper and deeper into the crypt of the family castle. Each time the host asks, 'Are you sure you don't want to go back?' the guest tells him to lead on. The guest ignores the cold, damp air of the place because he's drunk and trusting and curious. And he's dressed as a fool or jester, in a cap with bells. Students get it."

"It's one of your favorite stories, isn't it, Athena?" asked Kip, my boss. She was almost openly laughing at me. "This is interesting. What's your favorite part?"

I felt as if the answer must be written on my face, or maybe in the modest cleavage that showed above my neckline, the little valley that led directly to my heart. I knew that I couldn't ignore her question this time.

I nervously brushed the long hair out of my eyes and tossed it behind my shoulders before I realized how flirtatious this must look.

"That moment when the host chains his friend to the wall," I told her. I took a deep breath and let it out slowly. Kip's gaze dropped to my small, perky breasts, and her smile widened. "It's so intimate. He fastens his victim's wrists to bolts in the wall that have been used to secure captured enemies for centuries. Then the host chains his victim's waist. They must be physically close for that, and the fool doesn't fight back at first because he trusts his friend. It's only when he realizes that he's not going to be released that he struggles. 'For the love of God, Montresor!' he begs, but he gets no mercy."

I shifted my butt on Kip's sofa, and she looked down at my hips in sleek black pants.

"It's horrifying, of course," I said, "but think about it: Montresor wants to keep his old friend there forever, with the bones of his own ancestors. No one makes commitments like that anymore." I was trying to lighten the mood. I thought I sounded young and foolish.

"So you think the story has a homosexual subtext?"

"Yes," I told her, forcing myself to look into her shrewd chocolate-colored eyes. "No one names it, but it's there."

"And the act of chaining someone up seems erotic to you?" she demanded. "Or would you rather be the helpless victim? The one who gets shackled or fettered in a dungeon by one who lured you down there by offering you something special?"

For the love of God! She had led me to this point in the conversation, and I had willingly followed. And now I couldn't find a graceful way to go back or get away. "Uh," I answered. "I'd like to be chained up." There. I had said it. "Not permanently, of course! Just for awhile. By someone with better intentions than any of the maniacs in Poe's stories! I'd like to be locked up or tied up by someone who wants me. Alive. Not someone who wants me dead."

"Gotcha," grinned Kip. She didn't seem shocked at all.

Oh yes, I thought. *You get me, you read me, and now you know you can have me any time you want.* I was tempted to resign right then.

Kip had more to say. "You tend to run away if you're not tied down, don't you, babe? I bet you'd like me to chase you into a corner and wrestle you to the floor. You can get what you want, my dear, but you have to ask for it. That's the rule."

I really hadn't seen this coming. Two weeks before, Kip had seemed unusually friendly when I was the last guest to leave her house after a department party that she had put on as an icebreaker at the beginning of the fall semester. Once we were alone, her strong, graceful hands punctuated her comments with taps on my shoulders. While I was making a point about the transvestite heroines in Shakespeare's plays, she distracted me by stroking my hair. While showing me through her house, she led me by the hand. I secretly hoped that she was planning to throw me onto her vintage brass bed, but I couldn't be sure I was reading the signs clearly.

In any case, my common sense told me that getting sexual with my boss would be a really bad career move. My moist cunt was telling me other things.

Kip offered me a brandy and I accepted, but nothing she said or did was a clear proposition. Finally, I thanked her for a lovely evening and stood up to leave. She followed me to her front hallway, where she calmly pulled me into her arms as though she wanted to dance. Before I could react, she tipped my head back slightly and pressed her lips to mine. When I didn't resist, she slid her tongue into my mouth. *Yes!* I felt faint, but I didn't mind.

I could taste the wine she had drunk and the salty peanuts she had eaten. I could feel her heart beating beneath her small, hot breasts. I could feel my panties growing wetter, and I wondered if she could smell me. I breathed in her own clean but earthy smell as I moved my hips, hoping she found me irresistible.

Kip pulled her mouth away from mine, and smoothly pushed me away from her. "I'll see you at school on Monday, Athena," she smiled. I felt as if she had just poured icewater over me.

"Goodnight. See ya," I muttered. I grabbed my jacket and pulled it on while opening the front door, and rushed out to the darkness. I didn't want Kip to know how disappointed I was.

In the following weeks, I told myself that she had done the right thing, and that I should be glad to be working for someone who was ethical enough to protect me from my own reckless desire.

But my dreams were so lurid and drastic that I remembered them clearly while showering, dressing, and preparing myself for my audience of students. A few scenes even jumped into my mind's eye when I was driving to work or grading essays or exchanging small talk with a colleague: Kip beckoning me to kneel at her feet. Kip, dressed in black leather, pinching my bare nipples while discussing literature. Kip taking an old-fashioned wooden paddle off the wall of her office to use on my naked ass as I waited obediently on all fours. Kip approaching me with a scary grin that said that she wasn't violating my rights, she was giving us both what we wanted.

The best and worst scenes from the cinema of my imagination were full of restraining devices: Kip as a member of the Royal Canadian Mounted Police (and very handsome in the red serge uniform), pulling my hands behind my back (not gently this time) and securing them in metal handcuffs before pushing me into the backseat of a police cruiser to await further attention. Kip as a vaguely Shakespearian guard locking me, a mischievous and disheveled maid, into wooden stocks in a public square. Kip as a kidnapper, tying me up with rope before covering my eyes with a blindfold and my mouth with a gag, the better to spirit me away to her secret lair.

When the real Kip had invited me back to her house for a drink and a private conversation, I had ignored my common sense and said yes.

But now she had really gone too far. "I don't *run away*, Kip," I told her. "Jesus. I can take a hint. You told me you would see me later, at school. What was that about? I don't stay where I'm not welcome, and you almost pushed me out the door."

Kip's smile never wavered. "I did no such thing, Athena," she told me. "You assume far too much. You need to be taught a lesson. You haven't seen my basement yet, have you?"

"No," I sneered. "Is that where you keep the bodies?"

"Not yet," she replied calmly. "I've only lived here for a few months. But the house has a history. One of the previous owners was charged with cruelty to animals for keeping his dogs chained up in the basement. It's an easy thing to do, not only to animals."

Now here was the rub, so to speak: bondage could be abandonment and neglect based on contempt. It wasn't always loving entrapment, delicious conquest, security, and clear limits.

"The foundation of the house is made of limestone, very picturesque. Do you want to see it?"

"Yes, Kip," I told her, trying to breathe normally.

"I think you'd better call me Ma'am while you're here, my girl. That seems fitting, don't you think so?"

"Yes, Ma'am."

"Speaking of what fits, I want you to take off all your clothes before we go downstairs. I want to see you all over, and I want you to be in the proper frame of mind."

"Here?" I asked, somehow feeling hot and cold at the same time. "K-Ma'am?"

"Right here, baby," she smiled. "Take your time."

Trying not to blush, I raised my top up over my head, revealing my lacy black bra. "Nice contrast," she told me. "Your skin is so pale."

I managed to unhook my bra and drop it casually on my top. "Ahh," she told my hard red nipples.

I stood up to unzip my pants, and pulled down my panties at the same time, to get it over with. She licked her lips while looking at the dark triangle of my pubic hair. "You've never been shaved there, have you, girl?" she smirked.

"No, Ma'am."

Kip seemed to be imagining the slit between my legs surrounded by smooth pink skin, completely exposed to her gaze.

After taking off my socks and shoes, I stood naked for her inspection.

Kip walked around me as I stood still, trying not to shake or twitch. She gathered up my hair in one hand and lifted it off my shoulders and back, giving my sweaty skin a chance to breathe. "Stand straighter," she told me, trailing a hand down my back and leaving gooseflesh in her wake. "No, don't be stiff." She tweaked one of my nipples and ran a hand lovingly over my butt. She released my hair. "There's so much that could be done with you. Wait here." She disappeared into another room. I heard cupboard doors opening, and the clink of glass on wood.

Kip returned holding a glowing hurricane lamp. "This will help set the scene. Stone looks better in this light," she told me. "So does skin. You will look luminous as a damsel in distress." She turned off the electric light, plunging the room into darkness except for a circle of light around her lamp. "Follow me and watch your step," she ordered, pulling me by the hand.

The steps leading down to the basement were rough grey wood, and they creaked even under my bare feet. The basement in lamplight looked so large and ominous that the square shapes of a washer and a dryer in a laundry room suggested torture devices waiting to be used.

The grey stone of the foundation was only waist-high, with gyprock above it. I wasn't sure what to expect, but I gasped when I saw two thick metal rings set into the wall, screwed into the wooden posts behind the gyprock. Kip was obviously a more experienced player than I had ever guessed. With a pang of jealousy, I wondered whether she had invited other members of the department down here for an unusual interview or meeting or retreat. How unprofessional! *If she does this often*, I thought, *someone should report her to the administration.* My own hypocrisy stared me in the face, and I almost laughed aloud.

Kip set her lamp on the concrete floor. "Arms up, maiden," she told me. The thought of being at her mercy sent tingles straight to my clit, in spite of my common sense. I raised my arms, but my wrists didn't reach the iron rings until I stood on tiptoe.

"You're such a little thing," said Kip, making it sound like a compliment. "You need something to stand on." She pulled a sturdy wooden stand along the wall until it was directly under the rings. "Stand up," she told me. As I placed one foot on the stand, she helped by possessively grabbing my nearest butt-cheek and giving me a hoist.

Standing on a wooden platform made me feel like a statue, and it brought my crotch closer to Kip's eye-level. I raised my arms for her, and she secured my wrists to the rings in the wall by fastening them with velvet-lined cuffs that were surprisingly comfortable. *This isn't very medieval at all*, I thought before I could stop myself. Was I actually disappointed? My common sense was in despair.

Kip seemed to read my mind. "Life in my dungeon can get a lot worse, girl," she warned. "I'm going easy on you because you're new here and I'm unreasonably fond of you. Best not to annoy me, eh?"

"I'd like to please you, Ma'am," I confessed. She smiled.

Kip wasn't finished. She pulled out a metal bar with velvet-lined cuffs at each end. *Fetters for my feet!* She locked one onto each of my ankles so that my legs were held apart. I could only guess why she didn't want me to close them. She stood back to admire her work, and decided that something else was needed.

"Chains," she said, as if to herself. She walked to a corner of the room, and pulled a length of chain from a large canvas bag. Standing in front of me, she was able to wrap one end around my neck, and wrapped the rest down over my neck, several times around my waist, over my sensitive belly, and between my legs. Then she held her design in place by running two little padlocks through the links at my neck and belly.

The cold metal on my skin made me shiver, but the more I moved, the more it rubbed against my skin. Kip clearly enjoyed my dilemma, watching me discover the limits of my freedom. I didn't want to risk knocking over the wooden stand because then I would be suspended from my wrists. I couldn't move very much without making things worse for myself.

"Get comfortable, my dear," grinned Kip. "You'll be here a long time." Panic raced through me before I reminded myself that she couldn't really keep me in her basement for days, weeks, or months. Someone would ask where I was. Wouldn't they?

"You need the cap and bells of a fool," she told me. "I interpret the word 'cap' somewhat loosely. Not that they won't fit tightly." Suddenly she had two nipple-clips in her hands, and she was reaching in between the length of chain over my chest to squeeze them onto my nipples. Each clip had three little bells dangling from it, and they jingled cheerfully with each breath I took.

Kip stepped back to admire her work. "Now," she addressed me seriously. "I won't gag you because I want you to talk. And I won't blindfold you because I want you to see. You should be grateful."

"Yes, Ma'am." The nipple-clips were sending a message straight to my cunt. I felt as if my juice must be dripping onto the wooden stand, forming a puddle.

"Are you attracted to me, Athena?"

"Yes, Ma'am." *Duh. She just wants to rub it in*, I thought.

"Then why did you leave my house so rudely and abruptly last time?"

"You drove me away!" I protested. "You said 'I'll see you at work on Monday.' What could that mean except 'It's time to leave'?"

"Obviously, Athena," she pointed out mildly, "I expected to see you at school during the week regardless of what might happen between us in private on the weekend. You weren't planning to disappear into thin air, were you? If you wanted me, why didn't you say so?"

"I couldn't invite myself to spend the night with you!" I felt as if I could dissolve into tears like some doomed character in Greek mythology.

"Why not?"

"Because you could reject me, you could tell me how pushy and immature and unprofessional I was, you could tell me I wasn't worthy. You could even fire me on the spot. I didn't want to risk all that."

"Ah. But you, and women like you, expect me to make the first move and the last move and all the moves in between. With no risk or effort on your part. And you want to reserve the privilege of reporting me to the authorities any time you can't take the heat of your own desire. Yours, not mine. You don't want to risk losing your teaching career because it's what you love, but you'd be willing to force me out for life, and call me a monster, a Grendel from the lake of unwanted knowledge, to protect yourself. Wouldn't you?"

Kip really looked angry. *Shit*.

Tears stung my eyes, overflowed, and trickled down my cheeks. There was nothing I could do to stop them. "Oh, Kip, Ma'am, I really don't want to backstab you." *Liar*, I thought to myself. "I just didn't want you to turn me down. I couldn't stand it. I'd have to see you every day in the halls after that, and I just couldn't stand it. I would have to find a new job somewhere else, maybe not in a tenure track. You have to understand."

Kip looked coldly into my eyes. "Good start, girl. In earlier times, prisoners were usually tortured to get thorough confessions out of them. The whole truth and nothing but the truth. Very few people will tell it all if they're not under pressure."

She turned away from me, and walked into another room. In the split-second after she disappeared from my sight, I realized that I would rather be physically hurt than left to languish down here alone until she might remember me, and decide to let me go.

Seconds and minutes ticked by as I heard muffled movements from another part of the basement.

After what I guessed was a twenty-minute absence, Kip came back to me. This time, she was wearing black leather pants, a black T-shirt, and a black leather hood like a medieval executioner. And then I saw that she was holding a coiled bullwhip, a long and vicious leather snake.

I felt my blood actually running cold.

"Watch," she told me. She backed up, taking measured steps, and then pulled the whip back over her head, and aimed it at the opposite wall. The whip cracked in the air before falling harmlessly to the floor. I was relieved that she hadn't knocked over the flickering lamp, but I was afraid my relief might be short-lived.

"Please," I babbled, "please, Ma'am, don't hurt me with that thing. Or anything else you might have. I'll tell you whatever you want to know, but most people don't want the whole truth, you know?"

Kip smiled at me, and she looked beautifully at peace. "True enough, Athena, most people don't. This time, I think we'll just resolve the homosexual tension that appeals to you in Poe. Would you like that?"

My cunt felt like the inside of a volcano, if a volcano could want to be penetrated down to its lava-filled core. "Will you fuck me, Ma'am, please?" I begged.

"Gladly, my little slut. What would you like me to use?"

"Just your fingers this time, Ma'am. I want to feel you inside me."

Kip dropped the whip and strolled up to me, as though studying an exhibit in a museum. Without warning, she reached up and pulled the clips off my nipples. "Oh!" I burst out, as the bells jingled a wild tune.

And then she pressed her mouth against my wet, pungent bush and sent her tongue on a scouting trip to find my clit. She sucked hard as two of her fingers slid into me with the greatest of ease. She tickled my cervix and stroked my inner folds and harassed my G-spot until I felt as if I might explode. "Come, baby," she told me. "I want you to come for me."

"Ohhh!" The sound of my own voice bounced off the basement walls as I breathed in the smell of kerosene and reveled in the feeling of cool metal sliding over my skin.

"Good girl," purred Kip. "I'll let you down now, so I can hold you close to me. But you have to promise not to sneak away."

That was probably the easiest promise I ever made.

A Mountain Man in Drag

By
PM White

The shoes were killing him. With toes like Hondo's, fat as overstuffed sausages and nowhere near as attractive, girl shoes were torture. It was like trying to stuff a watermelon into a damn tube sock. He got them on anyway. The pumps were black and shiny with little heels on the end and his chubby feet jammed inside them.

He sported black stockings, too, which pricked the thick black hair on his legs as if there were little tweaser-carrying gremlins woven into the fabric. With a black dress and leather coat, and a heavy glob of lipstick, powder, eyeliner, and God only knows what else, his wife declared him nearly done. No way would she let Hondo leave the house without the wig on his head. The thing was like a bowl of yellow spaghetti turned upside down – some kind of Halloween leftover she unearthed in the closet.

"You're not leaving without it on top of your head, Buster," Amber told him. "If you're gonna do this you're gonna do it right."

"Where's my flask?" Hondo reached for the nearby dresser, wincing at the pain in his feet, marveling at the heaviness of his face, as he sat patiently in a chair while his woman put the finishing touches to his face. He got hold of the flask and brought it up to his lips, deftly flipping the lid with a swift flick of his thumb. He usually chugged down at work while he checked the oil on a tourist's Benz, never in a black dress that made the bulge at his crotch stand out like a beacon fire at midnight. Except for occasional trips to the bar with old school buddies and those times when he bitched out tourists at the grocery store, Hondo did not go out in public. Habit and routine suited his world fine.

Everybody in town would bear witness to the bulge in his dress, he figured. He drank a hearty swig while Amber plunked the wig over his graying black hair. He sighed as the sweet burn of Seagram's raced down his throat.

Amber sure spotted the swell in his clothing. When she finally got the hairpiece adjusted, she yanked the skirt to his waist, rubbing his white cotton briefs with one hand while shoving the skirt to his hips with the other. His bulge pulsed into a meaty erection. Amber wasted no time slipping his cock out and jamming it in her mouth. Hondo repositioned her hair over her ears and observed the woman's face as it bobbed up and down on dick.

She unbuttoned her blue flannel shirt, leaving the bottom two buttons in place, and hauled her large breasts out of her bra. She jerked him off, sucking at the same time, while polishing her pink nipples into hard points. A moment later she pulled her mouth off his dick, a glistening line of saliva dangling from her lips, and put her tits to work. Wrapping them around his cock, Amber began to pump up and down until Hondo shot his load. It sure came fast. Cum splattered her tits and face.

"Maybe that will keep the lump satisfied," Amber smirked, wiping cum from her tits with her fingers and sucking them clean. "I don't want that to be the only thing people see tonight. Not after all the work I put into your makeup."

"The way things look right now, you're the man. Anything you say."

Amber helped him into the couple's beat-up blue Chevy as Hondo kept tripping over himself. She drove the beast, which was rare. Hondo had a thing for being in control. He simply could not do it in heels, that was all.

They roared down Route 66, into the few blocks of the downtown area, toward Fixpound Park. Anyone who fancied a long drive would have to head to Flagstaff to get one. Hondo would have preferred a long drive. There was no such thing as a long drive within the city limits of Trapper.

Crowds flocked the downtown sidewalks. Try as he might, he could see no sign of a local among the mob of tourists. One or two would undoubtedly be found inside some of the restaurants. *The owners, at least; they're locals.*

Hondo wondered if anyone could identify him in a dress, with balled-up tissue paper forming a well-endowed pair of tits. Within minutes they negotiated the three blocks of the downtown area and maneuvered into the muddy parking lot at Fixpound Park.

"I bet you'd give anything to be wearing your skins, huh?" Amber asked with a crooked grin.

"Where's my smokes?" Hondo reached inside his small purse. The girlish accessory had a picture of a smiling bunny on the side with the words, "I'm cuter than you. Deal with it," written over its ears. He came across his unfiltered generics and planted one on his ruby-red lips. Amber usually complained when he lit up, but she kept her mouth locked about it tonight.

"Your flask is in there too." She got out of the truck and sloshed through the mud to the passenger side. His wife wore a pair of hiking boots, tight jeans that showed all her curves, and the blue flannel shirt, buttoned low enough to exhibit her full cleavage, which still showed a few red splotches where his cum had irritated her skin.

The Mountain Man liked tomboys, as he often told his old high school buddies at the Sultana Bar after shots of tequila.

Hondo considered his skins, hanging inside a plastic dustcover in the closet back at home. *Those are men's clothes, those skins.* Made from beaver, coyote, and other wild animals, the skins symbolized a time in the world when life and death struggles against nature transpired daily.

Hondo was a member of the Trapper Mountain Men; he had been grandfathered into the group. His daddy was a founding member. The same was true for the family gas station at the end of Route 66. Hondo got possession after his dad passed on. Group activities never got his rocks off, but he was partial to the Mountain Men.

The group formed in the 1950s as a way to beget interest in the small rural community. By honoring famed mountain men, trappers, and buck skinners, the group wished to smack the city's namesake on the lips of voyagers across the nation. The scheme worked remarkably well in the 1950s. People liked Marlboro men back then; kids wore Lone Ranger masks and dreamt of riding horseback through the sagebrush hounding outlaws while their parents read western novels and bought cigarettes at places with wooden Indians out front.

Hondo had been one of those Lone Ranger toddlers, but in the 1960s. He loved westerns, loved the horses and the stout women who domesticated the men of the Wild West. He convened in the back of the gas station after school each day, glued to the family's small black and white television and absorbed as many cowboy movies as he could, even if it meant skipping on his homework that day.

In a few short years the Trapper Mountain Men became one of the trendiest groups in the entire state of Arizona. People lined up to sign on. Membership in the club became as fashionable as a membership in the Mile High Club, if not more so. The group got to ride in Washington, DC; they got to shake hands with the president, and even became Arizona State Ambassadors.

They were real men.

If only Hondo's daddy could set his eyes on him now.

The other dudes lined up on a stage. Men like Hondo, a couple not like him, but all dressed in girl's clothes, stood dumbfounded on a rickety wooden stage. No one said anything about a stage.

"I didn't think you'd come if I told you that you'd have to get up on stage." Amber smirked, hiding a snicker of laughter.

A few awkward moments later, he stood with the rest of the "boys," glad for the full flask in his purse. The announcer for the event, a skinny, balding man who made ghastly jokes and laughed a lot, introduced the gender benders. They were Miss Cancer contestants, the bad presenter explained, and they had one hour to tear through Trapper collecting money for the cancer research. After one hour, they were to report back to the event and hand over their cash. The dude/chick with the most capital won a trophy.

"Damn if you ain't fine looking, Hondo," said a voice next to him.

His comrade and fellow Mountain Man, Twiddy, clad in drag, smiled at him. Despite the fact that two of his front teeth were mislaid and another tooth was only half there, the man had no problem with his version of a "winning" smile. Twiddy wore no makeup on his face, though he did wear a black wig with a floral sun bonnet over it. He also wore a blue sequined dress wrenched over his jeans and white T-shirt. "You sure went all out," he continued. "How you liking those hose?"

The smile on Twiddy's face seemed bizarre to Hondo. His eyes held more than a straightforward question about his nylons. Suddenly it dawned on him. *Twiddy knows what it feels like.* He had worn hose before, though he certainly did not have any on now. He also seemed to know what Hondo was thinking.

The way they squeezed his skin, from his inner thighs down to his ankles, felt like the soft caress of a sweet woman. Twiddy knew Hondo kind of liked that feeling. Somehow he knew.

"They're okay." Hondo glared out over the sea of faces in the audience. He could feel beads of sweat on his forehead. Twiddy spoke in a conspirational tone.

"I got woman's underwear on right now, buddy. Ain't nothing to be worried about."

At that moment the announcer concluded his horrific preamble to the evening's festivities. The party of men dressed in women's clothing stumbled off the stage. Hondo made his way to the front of the crowd. A number of "drivers" waited to take the group around town. He ended up with a young woman from Phoenix named Tyra. She explained that her mother, from Trapper, got cancer and died a year ago.

"Where do I sit?" Hondo reached into his purse for his smokes. He slid one into his mouth and lit it as Tyra opened the passenger door of her black Hyundai.

"My mom died from lung cancer," she said, "but if you want to smoke, go ahead."

"Thanks."

Hondo considered telling her about his own father who kicked the bucket thanks to cancer less than six months ago. Instead, he reached into his purse for his flask. He became aware of the woman staring at him. His dress hitched up nearly around his waste when he climbed into the car. He sat "man-style" and neglected to notice that his white briefs were exposed.

"So what's your name?" Tyra averted her eyes and focused on the road ahead. Hondo introduced himself as he tipped the flask into his mouth. He smoothed his skirt and told her about his gas station and wife, who undoubtedly still had a smirk on her face as she passed the time back at the cancer event.

"Sounds like a good little life you've got here." Tyra smiled at him. "You going to share that flask or not?"

Hondo handed it over as they reached the first location. He tried to smooth out his bulge as they headed into the rodeo barn, though the harder he tried to hide, the bigger it seemed to get. A number of RVs and tents encircled the old historic rodeo building. A biker group had chartered the whole place out for the weekend in order to hold a minor rally. Mouths hung open as Tyra and Hondo went into the place. While exposed breasts, wet T-shirts, and keg races were fairly conventional fare for this particular organization, a man dressed in drag crossed a big line. The two entered the barn area, where a number of people sat around with beers, all wearing some form of leather or another.

A number of them, burly guys in black leather coats with steely eyes, got up from their seats to surround the couple. Hondo's muscles tensed. He positioned himself in front of the young woman that accompanied him. She would have none of that.

"Wait, wait, wait," she cried, marching out from behind the big Mountain Man's feminine shadow. "We're here to raise money for cancer! We're part of the cancer group! Guys dress in women's clothing and raise money for cancer!"

"Cancer?" A woman stood up from one of the tables. She appeared to be in her forties and wore tight blue jeans and a skimpy white leather corset with a tight black choker around her neck. "I've heard of this. It's kind of like a contest, right?"

The men stepped aside as the woman drew closer to marvel at Hondo.

"That's right." Tyra looked around at the bikers. She barely seemed troubled at all. "Does anyone want to contribute to the cause?"

Hondo watched in horrified silence as the crowd assembled to gape at him. They chattered like little girls about how charming he looked, how the black hose made his legs hot, how regrettable that his boobs were not genuine, and so on. Aside from revulsion, he could feel something else as well. He thought about what Twiddy said. *How you liking those hose?*

In the glow of the rodeo barn, Hondo got a better look at his driver as she amassed money from the bikers, who promptly warmed up to the sight of a man in drag. Tyra appeared to be in her twenties, with jet-black hair and blue eyes. She was as narrow as a toothpick and wore a black miniskirt that showed a lot of ivory skin and a white button-up shirt with the sleeves spooled up to her elbows. The outfit looked semi-male and semi-female.

It turned out most of the bikers were lawyers from southern Arizona. It made sense to Hondo, who had no funds for a bike himself. There were a plethora of gurgling Harleys in Trapper at any given time, but most called other cities home. Tyra handed the money to Hondo for him to deposit in his bunny purse. His face burned hot with embarrassment.

"They're paying extra so they can get their picture with you," she said, smiling shyly. "I told them you'd be happy to."

The woman in the corset went first. She dropped her garments to the concrete floor of the rodeo barn and approached the Mountain Man. The strange woman massaged her large brown nipples over Hondo's faux chest, smiling coyly as the bikers snapped photos with their cell phones and digital cameras. Hondo proffered a weak "cheese" as the cameras flashed. By the last flash, his cheeses got better. As a Mountain Man of the tourist Mecca of Trapper, he was used to having his photo taken, but there were no similarities here. Sexual vigor electrified the old barn. When he wore his skins and bore his black powder rifle, the photos were obliged and hampered.

Tyra asked to have her picture taken with Hondo last and handed her cell phone to one of the bikers. Her short stature allowed her to stand in front of him. Warming to his predicament, Hondo wrapped her in a bear hug.

Back in the car, Tyra chuckled playfully.

"You're still smiling." She waved bye to the bikers as they left the rodeo grounds. Hondo lit a cigarette and rubbed his hands over his legs. He scarcely detected the smarting in his toes. The tightness, the silkiness of the hose, overwhelmed everything else.

"I think you're enjoying this. Maybe for a guy who owns a gas station and likes to smoke and look tough, there's a feminine side to you too?" She stared over at her passenger. He stopped smiling.

Hondo leaned back in the chair and brushed a lock of plastic blonde hair from his face. He looked out the window into the shadowy night.

"It's okay," she laughed. "Don't fight it."

"I'm not fighting nothing."

"You make a great-looking, albeit masculine, woman. There are guys and girls I know in the valley who would pay big bucks for the likes of you." Tyra kept her eyes on the street as Hondo turned his head to examine her. *Who the hell is this woman?*

"I work at a place, you could say, where kinky is in. Where people embrace sexual awakening in whatever way suits them. I get choked a lot. Tied up in a bow."

"Sounds weird," Hondo said. He flicked open his flask with his thumb. Sighing, Hondo stared at her white toothpick legs as she rammed her foot on the accelerator. He liked more meat on his women, but she did have a certain allure about her. It could have been her clothes, half man and half woman. Amber had that going for her. She liked to wear Hondo's shirts, but Tyra seemed to have it down to a science.

"It's not as weird as all that. Everybody's into something. I do schoolgirl stuff and business woman stuff, usually for business men. I've seen a lot of scrawny white cocks more full of angst than sperm." She laughed and turned to smile at him. "I hope I'm not saying too much, but I can tell when there's a hidden thrill going on. You're making it pretty obvious."

Hondo swallowed. "Tell me more."

"Why don't you masturbate while I talk?" she suggested, while dropping one hand onto her crotch as she drove.

The Mountain Man hesitated, but only for a split second. He hiked his skirt up to his waist and thrust his white briefs down to his knees. His thick penis sprung out like a tent pole. Tyra peeked over at her passenger as she spoke, disclosing to Hondo stories of the men and women she role-played with on a daily basis while he wrapped his fingers around the base of his cock. Hondo disliked jerking off quickly. He preferred the protracted method, gradually encouraging the explosion of sticky white cum. Tyra rubbed her pussy through her clothing as she spoke, keeping an eye on the man in the seat beside her as he got himself off. His facial features were obscured. The crazy blonde wig hid everything but his chin and lips.

Hondo's orgasm shot like a geyser in the car. He gasped, arching his back in the throes of orgasm as cum splattered on the dashboard like whipped cream spurting from a half-empty container.

"That's a lot of jizz, buddy," Tyra said. "I knew you were digging this cross-dressing thing, having women control that big-ass manhood of yours."

While he did not win for getting the most cash, despite the liberal contribution from the bikers, Hondo did win the "best dressed" award. Twiddy got a mite jealous over that. His winnings were zilch. After accepting the trophy, a Ken doll dressed in Barbie's clothes, Hondo did a little foxtrot on stage. He even pinched his boobs and laughed at the bald announcer's bad jokes. Not that he thought they were comical in any way, but because he did not mind laughing at him publicly.

Amber's jaw dropped. Twiddy clapped his hands. Tyra blew him kisses from the audience.

Hondo squandered no time getting changed when he got home. To Amber's astonishment, however, it was not into his sweat pants and white T-shirt. He inquired about her dresses, the ones she wore on those rare circumstances that they did something out of the ordinary.

"And your undies, too, babe. Where are they? I want to know what Twiddy's talking about."

"Twiddy? My underwear? Are you drunk, buster?"

"No, I'm hard as a rock. Come here. And bring your spanking hand."

Crossed

By
Kane

Some things you never forget.

I'd spent the day in Bath, smiling at my cartoon self in the blood and the silk of the bridesmaid dress. My Mohawk fingered into femme, pretty, cuteness. It made me feel boyish and naughty. Like I really shouldn't be there, yet I was and I looked hot in my own mischief and grazed knees kind of way.

I remember it all. The changing room, the coffee, the tapping of my shoes in the sunshine on the station platform, waiting. The choice to walk home from the station in the white heat of a summer that turned shop entrances into the mouths of caves, gaping their cold blackness into the street.

You lived en route. I'd left my bike at your house. It made perfect sense to drop in, pick it up, and ride the rest of the way home.

I remember the shock on your face when you opened the door. I saw you for the first time. The shock turned to embarrassment as you ran in to pause *Desert Hearts*. You had been caught.

I had no idea. I didn't know you'd been fucking yourself all day and that young, breathless, excitedness was you. Vulnerable and fucked senseless.

And there I was. Ready to be your muse, the clay. You were tearing at the seams of your perfect life and I walked in just in time to be your accomplice. It could have been anyone. But it was me. I was clueless. I was sick. I was wide eyed and gurning on dance floors, blissed out and intoxicated, climbing trees and skipping over roofs at dawn with people who didn't know any better either. I was painfully young. I was the antithesis of your safe life, with your beautiful wife, in your white house in that green street.

And all this time, I thought you reeled *me* in.

I don't know how it happened in that conversation in the kitchen but it did. Easy words and belly laughs and hours passed. Laughing over each other, falling over each other. It got dark, we got drinks, we laughed into the night and we knew, even then, we were already gone wherever we were going, but for the getting there.

Sobriety and sunshine didn't make it go away. The pull of us was like hunger. Craving and clawing. Fuck everybody else. Fuck everything else. This is everything.

That phone call.

I want to know who you are.
You have no fucking idea, little girl.
Show me.
If I show you, there's no going back.

Show me.

You fucking idiot. Shower. Wear loose clothes you don't care about ruining and be outside your house at 9:30pm. Tell no one.

I opened my mouth in the shower, taking in water until my mouth was full and overflowing and I shook suddenly. I had no idea.

9:30.

You pushed me into the backseat of the car and handed me the shot of tequila. I downed it and returned the empty glass. Proud. That hard slap across my face stunned me into silence. I wanted to cry, instant and intensely. I wasn't going to cry. Black. The blindfold across my eyes. My hands tied fast. I was so terrified. So wet. You were fucking me already.

The drive felt like forever. You were mostly silent and when you spoke it was in gravel, aching cruelty.

You just had to push it, didn't you? I gave you every chance. You think you can play with me, little girl?

No –

Shut the fuck up! Shut that sexy fucking mouth of yours up or I'll come back there and smack it shut myself!

Fuck you.

(Your laughter)

Fuck you!

I think you'll find it's me who will be fucking you, sweetheart. Now stop being fucking precious.

The engine cut to silence. Thick silence. I was in the seat, and then I was face down and tasting mud. Flipped over and gagged, pulled to my feet. Mud in my mouth and the smell of wet garlic and grass in my nose. We were miles away from anywhere.

Suddenly I realised how little I really knew of you. Too little to play a game like this. Suddenly I saw myself; bound, gagged, and blindfolded with a near stranger, nowhere near anywhere, and no one knowing where I was or who I was with. I heard your voice from that call, "Tell no one." I had been kidnapped. I wanted it to stop. I knew I'd gone too far.

You took my hand.

Now you have to trust me. There's only me here. I am your eyes, your touch. I am it all. I walk away and you're lost.
Yes.
So you need me.
Yes.
You're fucked without me.
Fuck you.

The slap across the face. Hard. I tasted blood.

You're fucked without me.

Yes.

I hated you, I loved you. I wanted to be fucked, consumed, and beaten by you all at once. I wanted to give myself to you. To be debased and devoured and disgraced.

It was steep and you moved me gently around and over each obstacle that I could only imagine. Down and down.

You tore my clothes off. I stood naked, blind, mute, and shivering in the night. In the silence. You tied my hands and feet to something – bars? I was stood, tied, trapped.

This is it, little girl. I'm going to have you now. However I want.

You were behind me. The softest touch of your fingers running from my neck, down my arms, over my hips, down my legs to my feet. I shook. My breath came in tugs. My cunt ached. I could feel my pulse in it. You open your palm and push lube into my cunt and my ass.
    Then nothing.
    The breeze on the lube, like ice, my teeth chattered and I squirmed. I yelped with it, that lust, through the gag.

Then it came. Your whole fist. Pushing and punching deep inside me. I cried. I felt the tears on my cheeks and I screamed. You pushed harder and I opened. Snot and tears messed up my face and made it hard to breathe. I was yours, I was just yours.

You shoved two fingers into my ass and fisted me and swore.

You fucking cunt. You stupid bitch. Stop crying, little girl! You asked for it! You begged for it!

I tore and I bled and I came, and again. I shook. And you did whatever you wanted.

At once I was empty. Alone. Silence, thick again, filling my ears like water.

A light touch on my back, like a gentle brush. Then cold, and then a burning pain, hot in my head and ringing in my ears.

I'm cutting you.

Cold water over my head, immediate and terrifying.

Then you were my parent. Washing me down. My snotty face. My bloody back. My ruined ass and cunt.

The warmth and comfort of my clothes as you wrapped them softly back over my shaking body. Me, crying and euphoric.

That's right. Arm up. Yes. Well done. You're so beautiful. You're safe now. I'm taking you home.

I don't remember the drive home. I remember blinking into your face as the blindfold came off. That love in your face. The tears ambling lazily over your cheeks. The breathed *I love you's* and the goodbye we both knew was permanent.

It was almost dawn as I stood in the bathroom, this familiar place and saw myself in the mirror. My face had changed. I didn't recognise myself. I looked touched, marked, moved someplace else and forever.

I pulled my T-shirt over my head and arched my body round to look at the cuts in my back. A pattern. Two arrows. Perpendicular and point in opposite directions. So close, one and the same, but never coming together.

Shattered Glass

By
Jerry Rosen

Miss Violet was tall, slender as a whip, twenty-eight, and looked it. Mr. Blue was pleasant-faced, some might even say handsome, fifty-eight, and looked every bit of it. You didn't have to be some Albert Einstein math genius to calculate the age gap which stretched between them like a chasm. It was plain enough for all to see.

Furthermore, you wouldn't be telling the absolute truth if you didn't acknowledge that seeing the two of them together made your skin start to crawl, if only just a smidgen. For while it was somewhat disturbing to observe them in public, sitting close in cozy booths in darkened restaurants, clubs, and bars, necking with abandon, hips smashed together like a car wreck, hands crawling up and down each other's thighs, it was creepier still to imagine what they got up to when they were alone, beyond the realm of prying eyes.

Nevertheless he was her dreamboat and she was the greatest piece of ass he'd ever known in his whole fucking life.

They'd met at a neighborhood coffeehouse. It was the busy hour. A great line of customers snaked back from the register. Harried commuters, already late for work, dumped packages of Sweet'N Low into their nonfat no-foam lattes. Children slyly extricated themselves from their mothers' grasp in an effort to roam unencumbered. And above it all, soaring with the angels, Howlin' Wolf, his gravely throat-singing voice sounding like a million shards of shattered glass, warned in a low moan that a mean ole black cat was just about to cross his path in the graveyard at midnight.

As was his habit, Mr. Blue was buried deep in the New York Times. It was an ordinary news day. In other words, the world was an appalling mess: government scandals, incompetence, and ethical violations; military insurgencies and counter insurgencies; ecological destruction on a scale too vast to comprehend; corporate greed, profligacy, corruption, and economic disaster. And in a faraway place, a war was being prosecuted and that felt really weird. But not now. Not in here.

Amid the bustle and hustle Miss Violet, though he didn't yet know her name, dropped a piece of yellow-lined notepaper onto Mr. Blue's table. She did it so surreptitiously he didn't even notice. By the time he lifted his gaze from the op-eds, all that remained was a taut ass that looked like a million bucks in a pair of tight jeans, sashaying serenely out the door.

The handwriting was neat and precise, devoid of even the merest trace of feminine ornamentation. Mr. Blue read what she'd written.

"There you are. Seated in the corner underneath the skylight. A weightless shaft of sunbeams pouring down like honey on your shoulders.

"You're almost hidden behind the counter which dispenses the creams and sugars and fake creams and fake sugars. But you don't strike me as fake at all. In fact, just the opposite. I think you might be the rarest of the rare: the real thing.

"Meticulously close-cropped pepper-and-salt hair. (More salt than pepper but who cares!) A tidy trimmed moustache, the kind you (unfortunately) don't see around too much anymore. Good upright posture. Lithe. Dark 501 Blues. Pressed white shirt. Strong hands.

"The kind of man a little girl is elated to meet when she breaks down on the highway at night or gets lost in foreign city. The kind of Daddy whose lap you want to crawl up onto when you've been naughty or even if it's just your period and you're feeling all blubbery inside.

"I can't ever remember experiencing such a strong presence from a complete and total stranger. I feel like the proverbial fly drawn to the spider's web, the trusting moth lured to the fire's magnetic white-hot flame. So I'll just confess and get it over with: I want to get to know you, to be close enough that I smell your scent everywhere all over my skin. I think that would put me into orbit, right up on cloud nine, in seventh heaven, completely over the moon."

Two weeks passed before Mr. Blue saw her again.

Without a hint of warning, Miss Violet stood beside Mr. Blue's table, turning up as mysteriously as she'd vanished the time before.

Mr. Blue gave her an unhurried going over, thoroughly enjoying what he saw. He started at the summit: the black beret which sat atop her lilac-tinted hair. Then he worked south. Face like a slumming angel. Tits out to here. Her long-sleeve T-shirt had a picture of a heart pierced by an arrow. Three teardrops of crimson blood dripped mournfully from the arrow's pointed tip. A narrow golden scroll with "Daddy" written across it in flowery script encircled the heart. At the base of the T-shirt's right sleeve was the word "Love;" at the base of the left, "Hate." She teetered precariously on a pair of transparent clickety-clackedy high heels. Those crazy stilettos didn't appear structurally stable enough to support anyone in an upright position for very long. In fact, she looked like she might lose her balance and topple over and crash at any moment! Did she know? Did she care? She projected an air of reckless abandon, an aura of erotic mystery.

"Did you read my note?" Miss Violet asked.

Mr. Blue nodded in reply.

"Then why don't we go back to my place," she said. "It's not far from here. My toenails need painting."

What are you like when you're stoned, Mr. Blue wondered.

That was then, this is now. And right now, this very moment, not for the first time or the second or even the tenth, Miss Violet was naked, ankles and wrists chained to the voluptuous "S" loops of a handcrafted bentwood rocker. Such a refined combination of form and function, thought Mr. Blue. He was down on his knees, holding Miss Violet's elegant, graceful feet in his generous hands. He'd just brushed on two coats of Vamp and the glossy crimson-black polish was still slightly tacky to the touch. So Mr. Blue lowered his head until his pursed lips were about two inches from the wiggly toes. In rapid succession, he produced ten gusty puffs, one for each slender piggy. But he did it with such care, such devoted tenderness and precision, that one couldn't help but be reminded of a virtuoso performer expertly navigating the musical scale. Finally, bending lower still, as far as he was able, Mr. Blue kissed the delectable freckle which resided so unobtrusively on Miss Violet's left big toe.

She looked at him with wide beseeching eyes. "Let's do something truly mean and nasty today, Daddy. Something irresponsible and half-baked. Something that will make me feel ever so dirty. The sky is like ashes...tear me apart. The sky is like lead...break me into a thousand little pieces. Then give me your benediction and put me back together again."

For a moment neither spoke. Then Mr. Blue said, "The poet Rainer Maria Rilke once remarked that in your darkest moments you shouldn't blame your life. Instead, you should blame yourself for not being able to see the poetry."

"What's that mean, Daddy?"

"It means I'm going to give you a gift, an opportunity to glimpse the poetry. But you're going to have to hold on tight."

Mr. Blue went to the kitchen. After hunting through the crowded cabinets, he removed a crystal wine glass. The round base and thin stem were pure dazzling white. The outer face of the elongated oval bowl was cut in a radiating pattern designed to mimic the delicate petals of a flower. On the interior surface, alternating bands of soft bluish-purple, the pastel hue of flowering wisteria vines, completed the effect.

Mr. Blue held the glass aloft to check if it was clean. By chance, a glimmering ray of light was intercepted and instantly transformed into a vivid rainbow, the result of the glass's prism-like properties. Perfect, thought Mr. Blue. It shines like a beacon. Still, he took a white linen dish towel and quickly wiped the glass both inside and out.

Returning to the bedroom, Mr. Blue released Miss Violet from the heavy chains which constrained her movements and bound her to the chair. He raised the wine glass for her careful inspection.

"In a traditional Jewish wedding," Mr. Blue said, "the most dramatic moment occurs just as the ceremony concludes. At 'Congratulations, you may now kiss your bride!' the groom stomps his foot to smash a glass and the matrimonial couple engage in their initial kiss as husband and wife. It's an exuberant expression of luck and joy.

"Now breaking anything, much less glass, generally isn't regarded as a precursor to good fortune. But Jews make an exception. There are numerous interpretations of the symbolism of this eccentric custom.

"Many say it's a reminder that relationships are fragile as glass. A glass, once broken, enters a state from which it can never reemerge. You can't, when all is said and done, put shattered glass together again, just as it was before. So it is with relationships. A single thoughtless deed, an act of uncommon cruelty, a breach of trust, an infidelity, and the relationship can be damaged irrevocably, broken beyond repair."

Mr. Blue scrutinized Miss Violet's face as he spoke. She listened intently, uttering not a single word in response. Her expression remained unchanged, an exquisite blank. After a slight pause to clear his throat, Mr. Blue continued.

"Some suggest a psychosexual significance that breaking the glass represents the sexual consummation of the marriage, the breaking of the hymen. Others offer a somewhat whimsical anthropological interpretation, that this is the last time the groom gets to put his foot down.

"More poetic or mystical explanations exist too. For instance, it's said that during creation, God concentrated all the divine light of the universe and enclosed it in a small glass vessel. He did this to leave room for what was to come. But the light couldn't be contained, even by God. The light expanded and, as it did, it shattered the glass, sending holy sparks flying willy-nilly in every conceivable direction, like a fantastic sparkler in a cosmic fireworks display. Today those sparks remain concealed, ensnared in shards of glass. It's as if they're waiting through all eternity to be liberated by acts of love, compassion, kindheartedness, and tender concern for others."

Mr. Blue reached out and with genuine affection helped Miss Violet rise from the rocker on which she'd been seated. She wobbled momentarily before regaining her balance, stiff from having sat for so long in a single unchanging position.

"Kneel down," Mr. Blue said, "and put your hands behind you."

Mr. Blue then wrapped the wine glass snug inside the towel and placed it on the floor in front of the obedient Miss Violet. Without hesitation, he stomped it under his heavy boot with all the force he could muster. The muffled sound of exploding glass was like the burst of a miniature grenade.

With great care, Mr. Blue unwrapped the towel. Splinters of broken glass lay upon it all in a jumble, each razor-sharp sliver glinting like a tiny treacherous diamond.

Miss Violet didn't have to be told to remain as she was while Mr. Blue left the room to gather what was needed to proceed.

"Bend over," Mr. Blue instructed when he returned. "Hold your arms straight out to the sides, elbows locked, and keep your palms turned downward." She looked like a beautiful diver perched on the edge of a high board ready to soar into the inscrutable unknown. Except that her face was positioned eighteen inches from the floor, directly over a menacing pile of broken glass.

Mr. Blue placed a small shot glass on the back of each of Miss Violet's outstretched hands. He filled each glass nearly to the brim with a rich amber-colored liquid.

"This is my favorite ale," he said. "It's brewed within the walls of a Trappist monastery under the strict control of Trappist monks. It's very expensive and very difficult to find in stores and this is my very last bottle. So if you spill it, even a drop, I'm going to push your face down into the glass."

Miss Violet kept her trap shut and her thoughts to herself, concentrating with all her might on maintaining equilibrium and balancing the nearly overflowing shot glasses.

Mr. Blue picked up a stick of butter and unwrapped it from its paper casing.

"The package says this is 100% pure sweet cream butter," he said as he smeared a thick greasy coat onto the fingers of his right hand. "With no artificial ingredients added. And that makes it even more delicious. Now that's good because I know you don't really like to take things up your butt all that much and I do want this to be as delicious for you as possible. Well, here goes."

With a single motion, Mr. Blue slid his index finger into Miss Violet's tender asshole. It went in to the hilt without a trace of resistance. He wiggled it around for a while and soon Miss Violet's breathing began to grow more labored. Her outstretched arms, however, remained rigid as steel beams.

"That was easy as pie," Mr. Blue said. "So let's go for two." The supple rim of Miss Violet's ripe hole expanded to accommodate the second digit. There was the faint beginning of a quiver in her outspread arms. The surface of the tawny liquid in the shot glasses was no longer flat and smooth.

"Now let's really have some fun," Mr. Blue said. "But remember what happens if you spill, even a drop." He inserted his ring finger into Miss Violet's compliant and increasingly distended backside, which had begun to sway to and fro like a pendulum. She was making a muted but steady humming sound, almost as if she was singing a lullaby inside her head to soothe herself.

"That's three," Mr. Blue said, twisting his hand in a corkscrew motion. "Three musketeers. All for one and one for all. Must be getting kind of crowded in there. See what you can accomplish when you set your mind to it."

Mr. Blue could see the beads of sweat which popped out like boils all along Miss Violet's silken haunches. Her face had become a contorted mask of intense concentration. The hum which issued from her parted lips had undergone a metamorphosis too. Just as the shaggy caterpillar emerges from its cocoon an exquisite butterfly, Miss Violet's song had changed in form and structure into something quite different, more reminiscent of a chant or prayer ... mercy, compassion, hope, strength, faith, absolution, a state of grace. What was this new music? We don't have a name for it.

Miss Violet's arms felt heavy as stone. The shot glasses shuddered and jumped around like a pair of excited jitterbuggers at a hot summer dance. Awful dollops of ale surged over the sides of both glasses simultaneously and, as if in slow motion, cascaded to the floor with sucking splats.

At this very instant, Mr. Blue grabbed Miss Violet forcefully by her hair. But rather than smash her handsome face down into the waiting glass, he yanked her head in the opposite direction and kissed her violently on the mouth.

Lucky

By
Xan West

I need to be forced to name my desires. I need to look them in the eye and accept them for mine. I need to travel that long journey through shame into pride. I am lucky to have someone willing to give that to me, who can go to those scary places with me. I am lucky to have Sir.

Sir knows me. Knows what I want. Knows where the edges are, and how to take me there. We go for intensity, and it is glorious, and scary, and cathartic. It would not work between strangers. It would not work if Sir didn't communicate my worth (and her love for me) in small daily ways.

At the leather conference, Sir dressed me in the morning. I knelt and she wrapped my wrists in cuffs. She had me wiggle into a garter belt, and then sit on the bed, as she slowly rolled fishnet stockings up my legs, and attached the garters, her fingers teasing my thighs. She pulled me to my feet, produced a skirt, and slid it up my legs, smiling with satisfaction when it barely covered my ass, leaving just enough bare thigh to show off the garters.

She removed the A-line shirt she wore the day before and through the night, and slipped it over my head, tugging it down my large frame. It smelled like her, of sweat and cologne and that musky scent that is Sir. She pulled out a deep-red lipstick, painted my lips with it carefully, and then smiled wickedly and wrote something in lipstick on the shirt. She handed me my Frye boots and ordered me to polish them and put them on. She was in and out of the shower before I was done, and pulling on her socks just as I finished. Her boots were gleaming, polished first thing that morning, and I helped her into them, my eyes lingering on the sight.

She unzipped her fly and pulled out her cock, saying huskily, "C'mere, slut," as she grabbed me by the hair and thrust my mouth onto her cock. I shuddered, feeling her deep in my throat, her hands fisted in my hair, fucking my mouth. She reached into me and named that core truth I rail against. I am a slut. I was helpless to ignore it with her dick in my mouth, and that was the point. I spend so much time resisting my own desire; those moments are when I can surrender to it, because she loves it, because it is safe, because I ache to so badly.

"That's my slut. I know how much you love getting your mouth fucked by me. This is who you are, slut. A hole aching to be fucked."

She thrust into my mouth quickly, grunting her pleasure, and then yanked my mouth off by the hair.

"Plant yourself on my boot, slut. Get it nice and wet."

My eyes lifted and begged her not to make me do this.

"Get to it, slut," she said gruffly, no mercy in her eyes.

I spread my legs and wrapped them around her boot, my cunt spasming as it contacted the leather. I was so ashamed that this turned me on. And so grateful that she made me face it.

"Ride that boot for me."

I thrust onto her boot, tears forming, pleading whimpers sliding out of my mouth.

"That's my good slut. That's it, ride out your pleasure on my boot. Don't stop riding it, baby. Open your eyes, let me see. You love this, don't you? I can see it in your eyes. You love being my good little boot slut. You can't stop until you cum for me. I want your cum on my boot all day, just waiting for your tongue to lick it up tonight."

Incoherent begging sounds emerged from my throat as I rode her boot. I knew the rules but I couldn't form the words. I couldn't stop fighting this. I battle in my head, every time. That's the point.

"That's my good slut. You love fucking yourself on my boot, don't you? I can smell you, slut. All day I'm going to smell you on my boot, and know you are mine."

My clit jolted, my cunt ached to be filled. Tears rolled down my face. I was ashamed and aroused and so fucking helpless. There was only one way to end this.

"Please Sir. Please may I cum for you, Sir?"

"I need you to say it, slut. Tell me you are my slut, and you may cum."

I could feel my eyes get huge. There was a lump in my throat. She gripped me by the hair tightly and her voice was ferocious as she said over my whimpers, "Tell me. Tell me who you are."

"I am your slut," I whispered, and her hands released me as I came for her, writhing on her boot, tears rolling down my face, my cunt throbbing. There is no release like tears and orgasm combined, and she doesn't forget that. She lifted me to my knees and gently licked the tears from my cheeks.

"Look at yourself," she said warmly, lifting and turning me to face the mirror. My eyes were wide, face flushed, hair wild. My lipstick showed I'd been sucking cock. The A-line shirt was stretched taut over my large tits and belly, and was so thin you could see my nipples clearly, "slut" written across my chest in red. My skirt had ridden up and my cunt peeked out, glistening. The fishnets had ripped, and the tough boots made me look decidedly queer. She had marked me, her scent enveloping me, her name for me emblazoned on my chest, her cock still on my lips. I am not just a slut, I am her slut, and her actions crystallized that fact. Being her slut makes me powerful.

She tugged my skirt down slightly and stood behind me, pulling the lock out of her pocket and locking my cuffs together behind my back. I stood tall, and followed her out of the room, strutting, my shoulders back, my boots loud, my head high. I was proud to be seen with her, my handsome butch in leather.

All day she showed me off. The attention made me dizzy. A tall gorgeous man with chocolate-brown skin, broad shoulders, predatory eyes, and fangs peeking out from his wicked smile, admired my tits and growled in my ear, making my cunt spasm. A gorgeous Asian femme dyke eyed my legs as she talked to Sir quietly. Her boy, a short, square-framed Latina butch, licked her lips and winked at me. Sir kept a hand on me all day, tugging my arms back by the cuffs to push my tits out further, stroking the back of my neck, resting her boot on my thigh as I sat at her feet. Her touch casually claimed me, keeping my arousal high.

Late in the day, she brought me over to watch a pale redheaded trans-boy black the boots of a gorgeous bear of a man with pale skin, covered in gray fur. She unclipped my wrists, massaged my arms, and locked them together in front of me, sitting me down to watch as she approached the bear to whisper in his ear. He nodded, gesturing to the boy, and they continued to talk, the bear's eyes grazing my mouth, my thighs, my boots. I was mesmerized by them, watching the boy's hands work, and when he lay on his belly to lick the bear's boots, my cunt jolted and my breathing stopped. Sir returned to stand behind me, leaning in to my ear as she pinched my nipples.

"Cum," she growled.

I did, trying to be quiet, my eyes locked on the boy tonguing those boots as I writhed in my chair.

"That's my good slut," she said. "I'm going to enjoy giving you away tonight."

My eyes widened. I imagined being given to the bear in front of me, my ass pounded by his cock. Or maybe his boy, using those strong hands to open me up. I could almost feel the vampiric man sinking his teeth into me as he rammed me with his cock. I could see that femme top holding me down for her boy, her nails raking my skin as her boy fisted me. I writhed in the chair, my cunt throbbing. I was trembling, my mind racing from one image to the next, until they all blended together and I met Sir's eyes, whimpering.

"Yes, slut. I'm going to offer you around. I'm going to make sure everyone knows how much you need to be fucked. You will be displayed for all to see. Everyone will know what a slut you are."

I was going to be displayed, naked in my desire. I shuddered, lowering my gaze. My clit was pulsing, my skin hot and flushed with shame.

Fear built through dinner. She sat next to me at a crowded table, as I awkwardly attempted to eat with my wrists locked together, watching my face as I thought about saying no, calling it off. I was not sure I could do it. I barely tasted the food, and sat quietly as the table ordered coffee, my hands resting in my lap. Sir leaned over and whispered in my ear.

"Stroke your clit for me, slut. You may cum as many times as you like, just do not make a sound."

I could feel the blush begin, heat racing up my skin as I reached for my clit under the table. I was sure everyone could hear the rings on my cuffs moving as I stroked myself. I gritted my teeth as I came, and could feel tears form as I continued to stroke helplessly. I came two more times before coffee had been drunk, and she told me to stop, dinner was over.

I was so hungry to be fucked I would have gladly bent over in the lobby just to feel something inside me. Sir took me to the public play space and detached my cuffs so she could put me in the sling. She clipped the cuffs to the sling and there I was, exposed. My skirt had ridden up, and I was spread wide, aching to be plundered. I felt so empty. She stepped back to look at me and shook her head, pulling out her pocket knife. She cut off the shirt, exposing my tits and belly, and then stepped back. It still wasn't right. She pulled out that very same lipstick and wrote across my broad belly. I couldn't see it, and I was stuck, there was no way for me to maneuver to read it.

She pulled her belt from her pants and stepped back, laying sting in waves along my upper thighs. She tapped my cunt with the belt and I yelped. Sir reached for something from her bag, fumbling with it, and then placed it at the mouth of my cunt.

"Please, Sir," I whimpered.

"My slut wants to get fucked, mmm? Not just yet. Don't you want to know what's written across that gorgeous big belly of yours?"

I nodded.

"It says, 'I am a slut. Please fuck me.' That's what you need, isn't it? To be fucked. By me, by my friends. That's what you love, to be spread wide and fucked. Say it for me, and I'll fuck you, slut."

She teased around my opening as she talked. I was holding my breath. She had actually done it. The fantasy I'd had for years. It was going to happen that night. I couldn't believe she had done it. She pinched my nipple, jolting me out of my reverie.

"I won't fuck you til you say it, slut."

"Please, Sir. I am a slut. Please fuck me, Sir. I am your slut. Please, Sir. I need to get fucked. Please fuck your slut."

The baton slid in. It was cold and excruciatingly hard. My cunt contracted around it, and it was so unforgivingly, amazingly hard. So hard it ached. Once it was in deep, she kept it still.

"You don't even need a dick or a hand to come around, do you, slut? You'd come around anything as long as it was hard and deep, wouldn't you? Alright then, slut. You may cum as much as you want tonight, as long as you make it loud."

"Oh god, Sir," I moaned as I came. "It's so hard, Sir."

"Yes it is, slut. That's right. And it's just the beginning."

She thrust it into me, and I came again, screaming for her, and it was still there, relentless, so intense that I began to cry.

"That's my slut. Cry for me. That's my good slut. Look up and see."

I did. There he was, the sexy man I had seen earlier with the vampire teeth. He growled in my ear and I came again, moaning. He had metal claws on his fingers and they traced over my skin. My eyes locked on his as he played me with them, watching me tremble. The baton slid out of my cunt and I whimpered as he moved towards my feet. His claws traced my thighs, ripped my fishnets, my cunt spasming, empty. Sir was at my ear, her hand stroking my hair.

"Tell him," she said.

I couldn't. I shook my head, my eyes closed, trembling at the sensations his claws were invoking. His teeth sunk into my thigh, and I came, screaming.

"Tell him, or he won't fuck you," she said.

I choked on shame as I met his eyes. They looked even more predatory. I felt so naked. I took a deep breath. He took out his cock, and it was beautiful. He put on a condom. I could do this.

"I am a slut. Please fuck me," I said softly.

He rammed into me. His cock was large and pulsing and so alive. My cunt clamped down and he groaned in response. He bent over and drove his teeth into my neck as he shoved into me. I was cumming in waves; it was one big circuit between his teeth and my cunt, building bigger and bigger. He lifted up and glided his teeth down to worry my nipple. I came hard, milking him as he growled. It went on forever it seemed until he raised his head and slipped out of me.

He moved to stand on my side next to Sir and I felt a slick finger teasing my ass. I looked up and the bear was grinning at me. He was sliding fingerfuls of lube into me and stretching my ass with two fingers.

"Are you going to say it for me, hmm?" he said, his voice lilting. "Are you an ass slut? I bet you are."

He winked at me as his delicious fingers enticed me. I could see his boy stroking him, keeping his dick hard. It suddenly didn't seem so serious. I looked up at Sir and she was smiling. The butch-femme couple approached, big grins on their faces. I was surrounded by smiling people, all delighted for the opportunity to fuck me. A weight lifted and the words came easily.

"I am an ass slut. Please fuck me," I said.

"I thought you might be," he quipped, and they all chuckled.

He gripped my hips, and eased into my ass. He felt amazing. The vampire leaned in and nipped at my neck. The femme stroked my thigh as her boy took my nipple in her mouth. The bear's boy fondled my other thigh. Sir leaned in and kissed me. I was surrounded by joy as I came. It rippled through me as the bear fucked my ass, and I could feel it gather in my stomach as it ramped up. He pulled out and gestured to his boy, as he moved up, taking off the condom and putting on a fresh one that smelled like mint. He slipped into my mouth at the same moment his boy entered my ass. He held my head still and they fucked me together. I came, screaming and gagging around his cock as it rammed into my throat. My nipples were pinched, hands stroked my skin. I was covered in sex, dripping with it, on display for all. I joyously thrust back against the cock reaming my ass. I felt so lucky. The orgasm washed over me as it built and built and I began to fly, weightless, soaring on pleasure.

The bear pulled out of my mouth and I could feel myself begin to laugh as my cunt closed on air and my ass clamped down on his boy's dick. I was surrounded by laughter, we were all laughing as we fucked and kissed and stroked. Everyone was touching and I was the conduit for all that energy, all that connection. Across gender, across orientation, we were sharing pleasure and joy and love.

"I am a slut! Please fuck me!" I shouted gladly for the whole room to hear as the bear's boy slipped out of my ass.

The femme pulled off her nails and slid on a glove, lubing it up. She stroked the edges of my cunt, teasing me with a grin, and then pushed three fingers right in. She leaned in and blew air right onto my clit, smiling as she felt me contract around her fingers. Her thumb reached up to stroke me and I came right there, moaning loudly.

"Yes!" I yelled.

She eased four fingers in, no problem now. That insistent rubbing built, concentrating around my sacrum, as she twisted her fingers, spreading them. She tucked her thumb in, working with me to slide her whole hand into my cunt. Her boy stroked my clit as she entered me. My breath stopped. I held Sir's eyes and melted into them, feeling the energy whirl between my breasts. She was reaching right into me, and it felt like Sir reached down to hold her hand inside me, right there at my sternum.

Sir smiled, and said, "That's my good slut."

I came, grabbing that fist, screaming, tears streaming out my eyes into my ears. Hands held me, I was cradled and safe and so so full. I looked up and the femme was kissing her boy. The vampire was smiling at me and stroking his cock. The trans-boy was licking the bear's nipples. Sir smiled proudly down at me and said, "I am so lucky to have you as my slut."

Her hand began to move inside me and the intensity grew in my chest. I could feel her pulsing, moving so big inside me. It was suddenly too much, and my leg started cramping. She eased out and I was taken down slowly, allowed to stretch. They took me to a nearby futon. The femme's boy was sitting there, her cock out, waiting. They seated me upon it, facing the room. She was packing a long thick dick and it reached into me, pressing insistently against my cervix as I squirmed on it. Her hands reached around to pinch my nipples and her mouth licked and bit at my neck. I writhed on her dick. It was so long, so relentlessly there. My muscles were exhausted, I was too tired to lift up, just stuck there, impaled on her cock.

Sir pulled out her dick and teased my mouth. I wanted her inside me more than anything.

"Say it for me," she said.

"Please fuck me, Sir. I am your slut, Sir. Oh god please, Sir. Please fuck my mouth, Sir. I'm your cocksucking slut, Sir. Please Sir. I am your slut, Sir."

She slapped my cheek with her cock.

"Tell me that again."

"I am your slut, Sir."

"Tell me that you are proud to be my slut," she insisted.

I came, riding the boy's cock, squirming, moaning. Her hands began lifting my hips, thrusting me onto her, moving me as she growled.

"I am proud to be your slut, Sir. Please fuck your slut, Sir," I moaned.

Sir grabbed me by the hair and rammed her cock into my mouth. I gagged, and she kept fucking me, smiling down at me, telling me to choke on her cock. Helpless, I was filled, my mouth moved by Sir for her pleasure, the boy moving my cunt to please herself. I flew higher, holes filled, senses overwhelmed, proud to be exactly who I am. Her slut.

Later, my mouth on her boot, belly on the floor, surrounded and stroked by those who helped her fuck me, I tasted my own cum on the leather and was certain that I got exactly what I asked for, precisely what I wanted. I lifted my head and smiled up at her.

"That's my good slut," she said gruffly, and stroked my cheek.

I am so lucky to be hers.

Halloween

By
Cecilia Tan

You wouldn't believe the stuff they do around here in the name of Halloween. Actually it isn't even Halloween. It's anytime. You walk into The Strand for their supposed goth night any Wednesday and you'll find stupid shit like fake cobwebs hanging above the bar and a lame little fog machine trying to make it "spooky." Spooky is a good name for a dog, not the atmosphere for goths. Or maybe it's just me. Twenty-one years old and jaded as fuck. Maybe I'm like those super-pious Christians, for whom Christmas is ruined by overcommercialism and hokey dumb crap for kids. Same thing, right? Halloween should be the goth Christmas, except who cares anyway?

So it was that on Halloween night I was at The Strand, sneering at a bunch of the newcomers who were slumming with the Halloween theme. Let's go hang out with the spooky vampire chicks. Fuck off. Go play pool or watch a ballgame or something. I was all in white to confuse the fuck out of them – the dress looked like a little girl's first communion dress, not like a wedding gown. Simpler, smaller. I wore a white wig. Some tourist asked me what I was supposed to be and I was going to tell him "a goth, fuckface" but for some reason I decided to take the high road, and told him I was Cathy from

Wuthering Heights. He replied he'd never seen that show and I wanted to beat him over the head with a book. Any book would do, but how about a nice fat one like a leatherbound edition of *Moby Dick*? Yeah, so I have weird fantasies, get used to it.

Micah was there that night, and Jeana, and Ash. All people I was desperately tired of. I resolved to spend most of the night on the dance floor where idiots wouldn't talk to me and I wouldn't have to listen to Ash mooning over some girl he'd never touch. But I ended up at the bar on the far side of the floor instead, nursing a Grand Marnier and pushing some stupid plastic spiders around on the bartop.

The guy next to me was perhaps the only interesting thing about the night, and only because I couldn't read him. People wear all sorts of stuff to goth clubs. We have the punks in chains, high goths in velvet, fetish crowd in latex and leather, and then on Halloween you can mix in a lot of other randoms in black. This one was in leather, but he wasn't done up like the fetishwear people usually were. It's hard to explain. He wasn't projecting an image with what he wore, unlike everybody else in the place. He was in black leather pants, a black silk shirt, a leather vest, and a leather jacket. He projected an air of ease, like this was what he wore every day. He was drinking water, leaning against the bar next to me, looking utterly relaxed and calm in the hubbub of the club. Relaxed, yes. Like he belonged there? No.

I guess you could say I got a bug up my ass about him. I set about tormenting him. It was pretty crowded, even on the far side of the bar so close to the wall, people were jostling past us, taking the long way around to the dance floor. I grabbed some kid I barely knew, Gary or Gerry or something, on the shoulder as he went by, just so I could bump into mister leather, step on his soft riding boots with my hard combat boots. "Sorry," I said in his general direction as I got back in place at the bar. I did a bunch of shit like that. I guess he had decided he had had enough when I ordered a water myself. I was perched on my knees on a bar stool then, and reached way over him to grab it from Dessa when she poured it.

My plan was to dump it down his back and play drunk, all oopsy, but as I pulled my hand back toward me, suddenly his hand was on my wrist, his other hand on the cup, pulling me forward off my tipsy stool. I didn't see where the water went but I ended up stretched out across his chest. One of his arms was under me, and he hitched us both into my bar stool, me flat across his knees. One elbow pressed between my shoulder blades. The other arm swept my little dress up onto my back, and then the flat hard side of his hand came down on my ass.

I was so shocked that for a second I couldn't think of what to do. Kick my feet and squeal like a little brat? Curse him out? He had hit me four or five more times while I lay there limp before I decided to slip out of his grip and just get out of there.

Decided. But he had that elbow pinning me and one fist wrapped tight in the excess of my dress. Four, five more smacks. Just enough to make it really hurt. Then he let me go and I tumbled into the legs of the people making their way past. Jaded fucks, no one even gave me a second glance. I climbed up his leg ready to give him a piece of my mind, but as I tried to get my feet under me, my fingers grabbing at his thigh, his hand was on mine. He slid it onto his fly, his eyes burning down at mine. I had the "w" of "what the fuck is wrong with you" already bowing my lip and instead I just stared. He moved my hand forward and back on the hard spine of his dick inside his leather pants, never taking his eyes off mine.

And where were my fucking friends to see this gorgeous fucking spectacle? Nowhere. No one was even looking. No one had even noticed. I narrowed my eyes and made my hand into a claw, squeezing him through the pants. His fingers went all the way around my wrist. Fucking hell. I should be kicking him in the shins right now, is what I was thinking, but it's not every day you meet somebody like that. I mean somebody who is just so outside the normal, so whacked out, different... I could feel his dick throb under my hand and his eyes flared a little when it did. You don't say no to a gift like that, to the challenge of which of us was crazier or more out there. My other hand came up and started tugging at his belt.

He leaned forward on the stool. His jacket swung open and he let my other hand go. As I got his belt unbuckled, his pants unbuttoned, I could feel the bones of his hips. Under that jacket I hadn't expected to find him so underfed.

His dick wasn't so skinny, though. I fitted my lips over the head and smeared my pearlescent lipstick up and down the shaft. Delish. I was down there in the dark, the smell of leather, the taste of it on the veal-soft layer of his skin, salty and sweet at the same time. I held his erection in my hands and swirled the wetness of my mouth all around the crown. The shaft was so fat, I couldn't get any more of him into my mouth.

Was I loving every second of it? Yes. Was I even then thinking of how to get the mother fucker good? Yes. And I knew how. I knew if I could make him come it would undo him. My feet were tangled with his somewhere under us, my knees had come to rest against the legs of the stool, and my head was completely hidden from the pandemonium of lights and music and fake fog and jostling that was The Strand. Just my mouth and his cock, my tongue working and my hands pumping at the same time since no way was that horse cock going any deeper. Wet. Hot. No air in there, really, nowhere in that damned building but especially not down there, not while

I was working. It was feeling like a bone in my mouth, like something supple wrapped around something else.

He was like a marble statue. He didn't move. Maybe he couldn't, jammed onto the stool in the crowd. If he was breathing heavy, I couldn't hear it. I couldn't hear anything, duh. I couldn't tell how close he was, and for a while it didn't matter. For a while it was like I wasn't even there, my whole body broken apart into sound and darkness and motion, like dancing, like those moments on the dance floor when the music eats you.

But I couldn't well forget myself completely forever now, could I. After a while I wondered how much time had passed with his cock in my mouth, fatigue burned my jaw, and I realized I had no way of telling how much longer it might go on. What was it I had thought when I had first seen him there? That he was hard to read?

So could I stop, would my pride let me? No fucking way. I kept sucking him, licking him, pumping him, the thump of an industrial beat through the floor keeping me going. Come on, mother fucker, give it to me.

His hand in my hair, jerking me back, my eyes aperturing open to see his again, his face close to mine, waiting for a kiss, bastard. He leaned in close, his mouth opening for a small breath, but never quite touched me. His other hand was getting his fly together again, dammit. And then he was pushing me into the crowd, his hand on the back of my neck. Where are we going, fucker? What's your plan?

The men's room. I should have known. You think it's the first time I ever sucked somebody off in the men's room of The Strand?

The truth?

Of course it was the first time I'd sucked a man's dick in The Strand. That's what I'm trying to tell you. This kind of crazy fucked up shit doesn't happen every day. If only. I was sick to death of the mundane crap that lurked just under the fishnets, the velvet, the tattoos. I wanted a bite of something weird and wonderful in life, I'd been looking for it for a couple of years – god, had I found it? It was my first year of drinking legally but not my first year of being a freak, after all. My heart thumped as loud as the bass as he pushed me through the black doorway, to the back, to the last stall and its door scarred with reverse graffiti, scratched out of the black paint with car keys and wristband spikes. He shut the door and I was amazed the latch worked.

The sound in here was muffled, the light dim but steady, but my nerves made it seem as loud and confusing as it had been out there. He knocked the lid down, and sat on it, his cock standing up again. He dug in his jacket pocket a second while I wondered whether I was going to get down on my knees on the damp floor or what. But no. He pulled something shiny and square out of his pocket. Gimme that.

I ripped open the foil packet of the condom and held it up in front of me, pinching the tip between my finger and thumb. I kept looking in his eyes and I can't really tell you what he was saying through them. Do it. Go on. You know you want to. It sounds stupid when I try to translate it. I rolled it onto that stallion dick, planted my feet on either side of his, my hands around his neck, and tried to lower myself down. Yes, I was dripping, honey heavy, and I got one hand down there and moved the rubberized tip of him back and forth along my wet slit. Okay mother fucker, here it comes.

I settled the head between my lips and sank down an inch and had to stop. God, so big. I backed off and slid down again. Just the tip fucking me felt nice, but two inches only does so much, for me, for him. I wasn't trying to be a tease. Suddenly I didn't want him thinking that was my game. "Okay, okay," I said to myself, to his ear, trying to get it deeper in. Oh god, this is just not going to work. Not like this, not this position. I tried to jam myself down, just get it in there and everything will be fine, right? Or would it? I felt like something literally might have ripped. I was frightened to look, but at the same time I thought, fuck, nothing bad is going to happen. That just wouldn't happen. It just wouldn't.

I kept thinking that. But I couldn't get him in. It hurt too much. And the friction right around the opening to my vagina seemed to be making me all the more aroused, and all the tighter. I gasped every time I had to pull off of him, until the gasps were sobs, and the sobs were me crying into his overlong hair, draped over his ears, my legs shaking because I could hardly hold myself up anymore, and I wanted to fuck him so bad, I wanted to lose myself on that prong the way I had when I was sucking him, but this time I couldn't use my hands to cover all but the last few inches of him, this time I couldn't be satisfied with that. "I'm sorry," I was saying into his ear, "I'm sorry, I can't, I can't, I'm sorry," unable to say more than two words at a time between sobs.

His hand on my back, bracing me, holding me, *hugging* me. The other hand moving his cock out of the way. He turned me on his lap then, my feet scrambling to catch up with the rotation of my upper body, until I was sitting on his lap facing the other way, his chest to my back, his cock sticking up between my legs.

His hand turning my head back so our tongues could meet, so hungry, so much wanting him. His other hand sliding in the wetness between my legs, his fingers sliding into me then, deep into me, long slender fingers so kind, seeking their way in, two of them it felt like, two merciful fingers, reaching into me, while his thumb or the palm of his hand or something ground my wet clit.

Oh my god, he was making me come. This is wrong, I thought, this isn't how it's supposed to be. How did I know how it was supposed to be? What were the rules? I had no idea, I just knew it was wrong. "No, no," I said, even as my body was beginning to shudder. "This isn't how it's supposed to go..." I was supposed to make him come, make him lose it, out there by the bar. "Not supposed to..." Barely being able to speak because of my lips still touching his, my neck still craned back, my chest still heaving with sobs. Off the map. Crazy. I cried from guilt, from failure, from how I couldn't stand the kindness of his touch after all that. But here it was coming, like a tidal wave, nowhere to run. He let my head go and I began to buck on his lap, his mouth at my ear, and I heard his voice for the first time. I couldn't hear what he said, but a shock went through me, almost like the shock of recognition. I think he was telling me to come, ordering me, even while his hands gave me no choice.

The come hit me hard, climbing up the front of my body, shaking me on his lap, bent back by his hand now on my throat, holding me to him. Wanting to kick my feet and squeal like a little girl. Or curse. Instead I just wailed.

When it subsided, he held me to him until my muscles started working again. He tore off some toilet paper and handed it to me and I wiped up the puddle that was mostly on him. I wanted to go home and cry myself to sleep and I didn't even know why. The pit of my stomach felt empty and I was dizzy.

I thought, fuck, I ought to just dash out of here right now. That's what I would have thought I was going to do anyway. But I wanted to hear his voice again. I wanted something more. So I stayed. So I stayed, and waited to see what would happen next.

He zipped himself up, looking at me the whole time. I had to look away, that staring, who'll blink first game... I felt like he could look through my skin, like his fingers had been so deep inside me he must have known what was in every nook and cranny. He reached for me then, his arms enfolding me, until my face was against his breastbone and his mouth was making soft sounds in my ear.

And again, his voice, his arms wrapped tight around my back, he said just one word, "Come," and my body writhed in his embrace, rubbing against the long spike of his body, my scream muffled by his chest, his jacket, as I convulsed against him. The sensation was like pain, opening and blossoming in my stomach but not a full orgasm – a quickening, a spasm, that left me still hungry. I ground myself against him, my whole body buzzing and shaking with the crescendo of coming, or almost coming, whatever it was. I slid my own hands along my thighs, and found my clit too slippery to handle, so hard and swollen I didn't know how to make myself come with it like that. I wanted his hand, his rough fingers, rubbing it raw. And I wanted to take that horsecock inside me. I wanted it and yet I couldn't bring myself to do it.

He loosened his hold and held me at arm's length. I was afraid he was going to say it again, order me to come, and this time watch me twitch helplessly without even his leg to rub against. Like I was under some kind of a spell. All he had to do was say it. I reached out my hand to his fly of my own accord this time, pressing my palm into the protrusion. I felt like I should be begging for it just then, but I didn't know how, didn't know the words, didn't know how this ritual worked. So I just rubbed him until he took a deep breath, and then carried me out.

He carried me right out of the club, and I smiled when I caught a glimpse of Ash jabbing Micah in the shoulder, pointing for him to look! He carried me to a small black car which beeped as we approached. He settled me into one snug-fitting seat, and then came around the other side and got into the driver's seat.

I don't even remember the drive. Maybe five minutes later he pulled into a driveway, and then led me by the hand from the car to a doorway in the back of a house. In the outdoor October air I could smell The Strand on us, the cigarette smoke and fake fog and sweaty sex smell, and then I was following him into the back stairwell of an old house, the smell of old wood and lead paint and the stairs creaking as we went up.

Inside his bedroom he lit a candle and turned on a small bedside light. I could make out shelves of books, small heaps of laundry on the carpet, but not much else. The window was dark and the bed itself was a mattress and box spring set directly onto the rug, no frame. I could almost feel a wisecrack about that bubbling up in my throat. But I kept it there. He had not said a word and I was not going to speak first.

He sat down on the edge of the mattress. And yes, he spoke first. "I want you to take off your boots," he said. I bent over and the wig, which had stayed with me thus far, finally slipped completely off my head, revealing my dark bob underneath. It took what seemed like too long to undo the knots in my laces, and then another forever to loosen the laces enough to step out of them. Now I was barefoot in that little girl dress. He stood up and let his jacket slip to the floor. I stared as he unbuttoned the silk shirt, undid his cuff buttons, and let it fall also. I knelt down to get a hold of his boot to let him step out of it. I don't know why I did. It just seemed right. Then the other one. And then I was helping him out of his pants.

Standing naked in front of me, he seemed no more vulnerable than he had when clothed. His cock seemed even wider because of the narrowness of his hips. From where I was on the floor it seemed very large and very close and I reached up to kiss it. Yes, I want it, I was trying to tell him with the kisses, the hungry nibbles.

He understood. He took my hand and we turned in place like a pair of ballroom dancers, and then he backed me to the bed. I sat down, which put my mouth near him again and I reached out with my tongue to suck him. There was the residual sweetness of the old condom, and the musk of him, making me tremble all over again. He was already steely hard but I sought to delay him another minute.

A minute, but a minute only. Then he pushed me back onto the bed, and wrapped my wrists in straps of soft leather. His voice was only a whisper as his body covered mine and it seemed to me like the words came out of the darkness I was floating in: "If you need to get out, say 'I'm not worthy' and I'll release you. Otherwise, I'll release you when I come."

And what came out of my mouth was "Oh yes please," which really made no sense. But it did, emotional sense. I quivered under him and he lingered there a while, kissing my neck, running his hands under the dress which I was still wearing for no reason other than neither of us had taken it off. Then he slid down to secure my ankles, my legs spread wide. My heart hammered in my chest and I examined the emotions flying around in the dark. Fear. I gasped and fear felt like an old friend. Little girl on Halloween night waiting for the ghouls to come eat her soul. His tongue found my clit and lapped at it like a cat, rough and methodical. His fingers searched inside me again and I found I could grind my hips despite the bonds.

And then he was leaning his bony hip against my thigh, one of his hands moving that tree trunk of a rubber-covered cock up and down against me, against my wet spot, and I froze. His hands coaxed me to relax, kneading my ribs through the virgin cotton of the dress, his lips on my neck again, the tip of him slipping in and all of me seizing it. My shoulders strained as my arms tried to hold onto him, but they were held fast against the bed. His face was above mine now, his eyes looking down into mine as he held himself up on his arms. His hips moved in a circle and I moaned, but he came in no deeper. I rocked my pelvis upward, and he slid an inch, like a seismic shift, two huge pieces of the earth being pried apart. My breathing grew rapid as I anticipated the pain, and I gritted my teeth and squeezed my eyes closed against it. But he held still. His lips brushed mine and I heard my breathing begin to squeak in and out of my throat. Terrified. Like that moment when you are hiding behind the closet door, and any moment the monster is going to rip it open.

He paused, one arm holding him up still as the other reached down between us. Those fingers, pinching my swollen clit. My eyes flew open at the surprising sensation, like pain but not a pain I expected, a shock. When I was a little girl I used to put clothespins on my clit and try to masturbate, and I could always make myself come. And then I knew what he was going to do.

"Come," he said, and my body began to writhe, trying to leap up off the bed, against gravity, against the bonds, trying to press myself against him. My eyes rolled up into my head and my sense of what was up and what was down faded.

"Come," he said, as ripples and waves of shock and heat and other things ran up and down my skin and through my belly.

"Come," he said, as our breastbones came together like they were magnetized, as his lips followed and I lost myself in the smothering sensation of his mouth on mine.

And of course, in all this, he had plunged himself deep and was somehow keeping himself to long slow strokes, despite my frenzy. When my spasms subsided and I could open my eyes and take deep breaths again, he was pulling himself within an inch of out, and then rocking forward, up my body, running the whole length of him into me until he was buried, and then starting again. We were both breathing deep and I felt like my insides were moving aside for him to let him go deeper.

"Fu-u-u-u-u-u-ck," I said then, without thinking, and he began to laugh. That made me laugh, like two actors on a stage who had just made a blooper – the masks fell right off, and all we could do was laugh.

"That's exactly what I'm doing," he said when he could. "You crazy little brat."

That made me absolutely squeal with laughter. I would have kicked my feet except they were tied down. And damn if his blood didn't quicken when everything tightened up on me like that. The next thing I knew he was tickling me, I was squirming as much as I could, laughing myself hoarse, half-orgasms flitting across me here and there, and then he wasn't laughing he was bellowing, gripping me by the shoulders as he jammed himself into me, one, two, three, four, five…and then he slumped. I think we both saw stars. And then it was over.

"Jesus fucking Christ on a pogo stick," I said, as he untied me. "Where the fuck did you come from?"

His chuckle was soft. "I could ask you the same thing."

"No, no, no, Mister I-have-leather-straps-attached-to-my-bed…"

"Was that your first time?"

"My first time, what, getting banged with a telephone pole? I guess you could say so." His dick looked big even shriveled inside the condom, which he wrapped in a tissue and tossed out of my sight.

"First time being tied up?" His voice went quiet and he sat on the edge of the bed, one finger trailing my arm.

I'm telling you, it was like a spell he could cast. A spooky Halloween bewitchment. It made my voice quiet too. And truthful. "Yes."

"Did you like it?" he said, even lower, even quieter, like music descending.

"Yes." I was trying to get my baby bitch face back on, but it wasn't coming.

"Do you want to do it again some time?" The quietest of all. I could only nod. He nodded back and lay down next to me. I rolled over and he wrapped around me spoonwise, pulling a blanket up from the floor with his long arm.

I could see then how it was going to go. He was going to ask me if I wanted to spend the night, and I was going to chicken out and say what he wanted me to say, "I'm not worthy," and then leave. Except he didn't ask. And I didn't chicken out. And we exchanged names in the morning.

Monitoring

By
Ralph Greco, Jr.

SMACK.

"Oh Lord!"

"Listen. Listen."

SMACK, SMACK.

"Anne!"

"There'll be more. Wait. Wait. There's always more."

"Are you a bad girl? Are you?"

"No...please!"

SMACK, SMACK.

"Lord, I can't believe this."

"It gets better."

"Tell me you're a bad girl. Say, 'I am a bad girl.' Say it."

SMACK, SMACK, SMACK, SMACK.

"Ohhhhh, nooooooo."

"Say it, or it gets worse."

"Anne, Lord, I can..."

"...shhh, listen, listen."

"Say it...SMACK"

"AH HA!!! Yes yes, I'm a bad girl. I'm a bad girl. I'm a bad girl!"

By the time Kathy and Anne managed downstairs both women were red-faced, shaking, and dewy between their thighs (though they wouldn't admit this last bit). Kathy had walked over for their biweekly sandwiches and coffee, woefully unsuspecting of what Anne was going to spring on her this day.

"I can't believe they don't wake the baby," Kathy said as Anne poured them two mugs.

"Well, they don't have to really be in her room for the monitor to pick them up," Anne said. "Still, you're right; they got to be close enough that she'd hear them. That kid must be a deep sleeper."

"Lord...and how the hell do we hear it over here? I mean you explained it to me bu..."

"...Bill says..." Anne began, passing her best friend the sugar. "...and believe me he had no idea why I asked; can you imagine explaining something kinky like this to my husband!?"

Both women giggled like schoolgirls.

"He said that if you happen to have a monitor that is the same frequency...same brand too, I think, and you're close enough, you can pick up other people's baby monitors."

"Lord."

"Makes ya think, right?"

"And you've never met them?" Kathy said fixing her coffee.

"Just to wave hello when we're putting the garbage out or something," Anne said, opening her refrigerator door. When she had popped her head back up and retreated from the big sub-zero, she held a plate of cold cuts and turned back to Kathy to continue: "They live two doors down, Steve and Joanna. Seem like a nice quiet couple, cute baby...who obviously sleeps through anything."

The women giggled again as Anne sat down.

"To look at them, you'd never guess he was spanking her and she was into it."

"This has got to be the wildest thing that's happened on this damn cul-de-sac since Emil Causing had that affair with their cleaning lady," Kathy said through a cautious sip of her coffee.

"I never heard that story. When was this?"

A half-minute passed as the friends reached around and through each other for cold cuts, mayonnaise jars, and mustard bottles.

"Holy shit! Holy shit! Holy shit!" Anne screamed seconds later, dropping her roll in mid sandwich-making mode.

"HOHOHOLY SHEET!" she added, grinning and sitting back in her wicker-backed chair. "This is Tuesday, right?"

"Yeah...what? What is it?" Kathy asked, grinning herself at her best friend who was obviously caught short with a recent realization. Anne's creamy complexion was now fully flushed from her cleft chin to her high forehead with whatever had just suddenly jumped into her mind.

"Her mom, Joanna's mom, takes the baby every Tuesday and Thursday."

"That explains why the kid doesn't hear them...or we don't hear the kid crying through all that spanking," Kathy said.

She was a bit too hungry though to stop making *her* sandwich.

"Yeah, but, what I mean is..." Anne mused, still bouncy as she settled her little butt back in her chair.

"...well you can definitely forget that a baby monitor is on," she continued, her blue eyes wide. "I mean we do it all the time with Lindsey and we used to forget with Billy. But what if they..."

"What?" Kathy said, halting the smearing of mustard. "What!?"

"I mean, there are a lot of moms like me home with a kid or two, you're the local divorcee, they'd know you're around too."

"You mean...oh, no, that's too perverse."

"Worse than him coming home from work at lunchtime to spank her ass?"

"My sweet Lord, they're doin' it on purpose with the monitor on?"

"I guess we're having lunch on Thursday, huh?" Anne asked and both women took up their rolls again.

Two days later Kathy and Anne were once again in Anne's airy peach and blue kitchen. It was eleven, still a full hour before Lindsey would be waking from her nap. From what was evident two days ago—and the week before when Anne first caught her neighbors at their kinky activity—Joanna and Steve began the spanking sometime about 11:45, giving Anne (and now, by extension, Kathy) a good forty-five minutes before Lindsey, the baby of *this* house, would start stirring. The women stood in Anne's kitchen now, their arms draped on the countertop, their faces all but pressed to the hissing baby monitor, stretching their nerves—and their libidos—for what they hoped they'd hear again.

"If this happens again, that's like two weeks in a row and we'll know for sure it's no accident that they le..."

I told you I wanted you to be in position.

Kathy and Anne turned to one another their mouths open.

I...I'm sorry I...

SMACK. SMACK.

Get those jeans down.

"Lord!"

"You said it, girl."

Good, good. Now over the bed. Assume the position.

I...

Do not make me wait.

"I can't listen to this," Kathy said, spinning away from the baby monitor and stepping to Anne's patio double doors. "Really, we're spying."

"They want us to hear," Anne said. "They are hoping some other monitor will pick them up. I just know it."

"Still, it's like being a peeping tom, I feel..."

NOOOOOOO. NO PLEASE!

"What the hell's he doing?" Kathy screamed, jumping back to the counter and Anne.

PLEASE!!!

SHATPA. SHATPA.

Please not the belt. Please.

You deserve the belt; you're getting the belt.

Oh God!

SHATPA.

"Oh."

"Did you hear that, her last 'oh God'?! She's *really* into this," Anne offered.

"Yeah but a belt?! Anne..."

SHATPA. SHATPA.

AH HA!

Kathy looked down at her crossed arms, trying to still her big chest rising and falling in her quick exhalations as the snapping retort of the belting continued.

"It's hot, right?" Anne asked as Kathy finally looked up at her. "I mean..."

"...yes." Kathy gulped, leaning back off the counter as four more belt swats landed with what she could only assume was a sharp sting. "But, really, Anne, it's too much."

She could just imagine Joanna's ass, the ass of a woman she had never even seen, reddening with little rectangles. Was the woman bent far over the bed? Were her legs tight together or did Steve want Joanna to have her legs open slightly, so he could spy her sex from behind? Was the woman pushing her pelvis deep into the bed with every swat? Was Joanna naked? Did she arch her back, throw her hair lightly down her shoulder blades when she took a hit? (Anne had said Joanna had long brown hair, hadn't she?) Did the woman dare look over her shoulder, watching in dreaded anticipation as her husband wielded the belt? And how about this guy Steve, the husband, was he standing their sweating with his shirt open or maybe even his pants undone? Was this Joanna looking at her husband's crotch the entire time he beat her, seeing his cock thickening with each connection? Did they both get so hot from this dominating thing that they fell into furious sex after? God knew, neither Anne nor Kathy had heard them having sex. It would speak to Anne's theory if Joanna and Steve made the spanking/whipping part of their play known, and then shut off the monitor after.

Kathy stood fully off the counter then.

"I can't listen to any more of this, really. It's too much," she sighed.

"You like it just as much as me," Anne snickered.

Nooooooooooo.

SWAP. SWAP.

"Jesus, he must have moved or something, they sounded different," Anne said.

Despite themselves the women moved close to the monitor again.

SWAPPA. SHWAPPA.

"Fuck, she's crying," Anne added.

"Ok, this is too much," Kathy moaned.

And indeed the belt slashes had been replaced by a low mewing, barely audible through the monitor, but there just the same.

"Good Lord!" Kathy exclaimed and shot across Anne's spacious kitchen. "We *should not* be hearing this."

"Wait, wait," Anne said, still leaning there against her counter. "Oh my God, oh my God."

"What?" Kathy reluctantly asked, still standing at the far end of Anne's kitchen table. It was as if she was fighting the pull of that little blue and white plastic monitor across the room from her. She was keeping herself here, close to the table, willing her feet not to move.

No, baby no...

"Oh my God, listen," Anne said. "Shit, she definitely likes it."

"Oh my! My!" and with this Kathy felt her feet move under her despite her willingness to stop them. She bit her generous lower lip and stepped gingerly to Anne and the monitor again.

I...I...oh God... God...I can't...

Yes you can...it's ok...you have been punished, you can.

No, please, not like this, please...please. The pain and the pleasure...

I know. I know.

Jesus, Steve, please don't make me...

Come baby, it's ok. It's time you come.

Steve...

"That's it!" Kathy declared, reached out to the monitor, and flicked it dead.

"Hon, what are you so bugged about?" Anne asked as Kathy stepped back to the kitchen table, reached for her glass, and gulped back some more iced tea. Kathy pulled out one of the six chairs and sat slowly on the edge of it.

"It's too much."

"I am almost one hundred percent convinced they want us to hear them."

"It's...it's not that."

"What's wrong then?" Anne asked. She walked to Kathy and knelt to her friend. "What's wrong? You can tell me. This is all in fun, really. You heard her; she likes it. And to tell you the truth, I don't think he's even hitting her that hard. Really. It's ok."

"I know she likes it," Kathy said, finally looking up from her big chest. "I know, it's just that..."

"What, honey, tell me. What's got you so upset?" Anne asked, placing her hand on Kathy's knee, imploring her with her wide blue eyes.

"It's just that...that... when I hear them, I... I really *really* want to be spanked to."

Anne stood, walked over to her liquor cabinet. They were going to need something stronger than iced teas to be sure.

As Kathy had suspected and Anne confirmed, Anne and Bill enjoyed a solid, respectful sex life, nothing kinky but satisfying all the same. And while Anne loved listening in on the spanking mayhem of her neighbors and admitted to a slight tickle "you know where," when they heard Joanna reacting so positively, she herself had really never experienced anything so kinky in her life before, or with Bill.

Anne was surprised—yet titillated—to hear that Kathy had had a totally different history. As the friends sipped their second Cosmos, Kathy told of enjoying a wild sex life before meeting Fred, her ex. Kathy's ten-year marriage had not seen fireworks in the bedroom—one of the reasons she wasn't all that broken-up about her recent divorce—and now that she was free to date and in her "prime" at forty-one, she had hoped she might revisit her more kinky times. Near tears, the alcohol buzzing her memory as much as what she just heard from Joanna and Steve, Kathy admitted to her best friend how she very much liked playing the bad girl, being taken across a man's knee, dressing hot for a night out only to pay for it later. With a torrent of admission Kathy's big chest rose and fell hard as she related to Anne how awakened her libido had been this past week with just the "idea" of what Joanna and Steve got up to two houses over; hearing them in the midst of all that swatting, pleading, and surrendering had made Kathy weak in the knees.

When Kathy left Anne's house an hour later, she was as exhausted by what she had heard Steve and Joanna get up to that day as much as she was by what she had admitted. And unbeknownst to Kathy, but certainly fueled by that admission, Anne called her mother that very night to see if she might take Lindsey for a "day out" the very next day.

Dressed in a tight knee-length skirt, black turtleneck, and modest two-inch heels, Anne answered her front door bell at twelve o'clock. Last night as she lay next to her snoring husband, she determined that she was going to see if Kathy truly wanted a spanking and at the same time see if (and how much) she, Anne, liked administering one.

As she lay there finalizing a plan in her head, Anne had had to summon all her will to keep from masturbating.

"H...hi," Kathy stuttered on the front step, obviously reacting to how sexy her friend was dressed just for lunch.

"Are we goin' out?" she asked. "I mean, let me go run and put on a blouse..."

"You look perfect," Anne said, smiling. She stepped back to let her best friend enter.

Anne had formulated, rehearsed, and then changed her patter again and again all morning. Considering what she would say to Kathy, how she was going to dress, and how she would act had her more turned on than she had been in months. She had never ever been with a woman in any sexual way...and definitely had never played the type of dominance/submissive scenario she was about to.

"You know you are my best friend, right?"

"And you're mine," Kathy said, furrowing her brow in confusion as Anne held her elbow and walked her into the spacious living room.

"I mean it's only been like five years since you guys moved in, but...sometimes I feel like I've known you longer than some of my oldest friends."

"I feel that way to," Kathy agreed, her light eyes dancing around the pretty well-lit room in nervousness. "I'm really glad I got to stay here after the divorce, keep the house and all."

"And you know I would never do anything to hurt you," Anne continued.

Kathy stopped looking around the room and stared at Anne hard.

Anne was smiling wide.

"I just want you to know..." the shorter woman said, walking her and Kathy to her low couch. "...what is about to happen will turn me on as much as it will you."

Realization suddenly hit Kathy as Anne sat below her. Anne lifted her skirt to mid thigh and pressed her pretty bare knees tight.

"I want you over my lap," the mistress of the house said, beaming up at her friend.

Kathy gulped, searching Anne's pretty pale face and deep blue eyes. Seconds ticked by like hours as each woman waited, poised and perfect, nervous and excited.

"You don't..."

"I'm not doing anything I don't want to do," Anne interrupted. "I know you want to be spanked. I have thought of nothing else the last two weeks anyway, and when you admitted everything yesterday, I was thinking, why not, I should spank you, see if I like doing it as much as I think I will...or as much as you *want* to be."

"Lord Anne," Kathy said, hugging her big chest once again as she stared down at the pretty thin knees of her friend. "I was pretty drunk yesterday; it was more the drinks talking than..."

"...I doubt that," Anne interrupted, cocking her head and fixing her friend with a kind, yet knowing, stare.

At that magnesium flash flicker of a moment, both women knew the spanking was going to happen. Kathy could have easily just spun out of the room and Anne's house, or at the very least, laughed aloud, pressed the point about being drunk, how Cosmos always went right to her head. She could have simply skittered out of the living room to go get some iced tea, chuckling at her friend's assumptions. For her part, Anne held her breath, poised as she was, trying to show a confidence she certainly did not feel, fearing any second she'd jump up and tell Kathy she had been kidding. Wet as she was, she was nervous too; Kathy could diffuse the entire escapade if she balked or even downright refused.

"You...you want me to just, just get over?"

"Sure, why not?" Anne replied, sitting back on the yielding floral couch.

"We can't just do this," Kathy sighed, her eyes not lifted from her friend's lap.

"Why not?" Anne asked. "Didn't you say you missed playing the bad girl?"

"Oh Lord," Kathy said, her chin dipped as her big chest began to rise and fall rapidly again.

Words like "bad girl," "slut," "my bitch," when spoken in the context of being scolded when spanked—nothing made Kathy crazier. A hundred memories flooded her then, of way-back-when sexual encounters when she was called any number of naughty names as she lay across a lap or sat with a hand sneaking up her short skirt. She was getting so wet just standing there; would she come the minute she got into position?

For Anne, to sit there, playing the waiting dominant, dressed sexy like that, about to do something she had never done to anyone, let alone a woman, was maddening to say the least...but oh so hot. She almost didn't want to look up at Kathy, just breath slow and *will* it all to happen. Would she ever be able to look at Kathy again and not think of this moment?

"Get across," she said.

Kathy took a step and came to stand at Anne's right side, neither saying a word. The friends locked eyes then, took a breath in concert, and then Kathy began to bend across the high pretty lap below her. Both ladies shuttered, wiggled, and sighed into their respective positions as Kathy gingerly lay down across Anne's lap and Anne scooted under her friend to support her.

That there had been a background to these proceedings, that desires had been discussed, particulars of their private pasts weighed and considered, made this all a lot less threatening. It was as if the context of the spanking negated all other possible considerations of propriety; Anne's marriage, Kathy's usual shyness, their shared resolute heterosexuality wasn't even considered with this most unusual happenstance. Both women had their minds wrapped around the procedures and positions of the spanking because of what they had experienced recently and what they had discussed because of it. This moment, for both, planned as it had been by Anne, sprung upon Kathy, would be nothing more than the spanking.

"I mean, this is not really sexual, right?" Anne continued as Kathy scooted her ass dead center on her lap. "It's more a curiosity."

"Well, it's still hot," Kathy said. She lay across Anne fully and placed her hands out before her, her long legs draped down off the other end.

"Yeah…you're right," Anne agreed feeling the heat of Kathy against her and her own little squishiness increasing.

"Just getting into this position…" Kathy moaned to Anne's feet and Anne reached back as quickly as she dared and *SMAT*, she connected her thin right palm dead center to Kathy's ass.

"Oh, ho, hrmm," both women sang.

SMAT. SMAT. Anne answered Kathy's exclamation with two more hits, again dead center.

"Anne," Kathy mewed to the floor and Anne lifted her arm, wiggled on the couch and began a succession of ten smacks, five to each of Kathy's cheeks.

SMACK. SMACK. SMACK. SMACK. SMACK.

"Lordee!"

Anne answered Kathy, repeating with five hits to her left cheek.

SMACK. SMACK. SMACK. SMACK. SMACK.

"Fucking hot, right?" Anne replied as Kathy straightened out again after the assault. Anne caught Kathy clenching and unclenching her cheeks through her jeans.

Her friend really did have the roundest ass, Anne noticed.

"You ok?" she asked.

"Yeah…yeah," Kathy sighed.

Lying as loose as she could again, she tried to ease her breathing and still her big tits rising and falling as she lay there inverted over Anne's knee. She was really wet now, but trying like all hell not to rub even the slightest bit against Anne's thigh. Anne felt the warmth, not sure if it was Kathy's or her own...and not caring one bit.

"So?" Anne asked.

"So?" Kathy repeated.

Seconds ticked by, both women stayed in position—Anne fearful of what she was about to request, Kathy sensing the question and aching for it to be asked.

"Gonna take your pants down?"

"Oh Lord, Anne."

"I mean, we're doing this, might as well go all the way, right?"

"I..."

Again there passed that snippet of slow motion decision both women knew would end in a positive outcome. Anne had known when she had formulated this plan in the shower the night before, as the water from her shower massager tickled her engorged lips and she grew ever more heated with the prospect of what she'd propose this day, that there would be no feeling of completion for her unless she bared Kathy's ass, smacked her bare hand to bare cheek.

Kathy only ever wanted to be spanked bare-assed. She had never been spanked any other way and the minute she lay across Anne's lap she was thinking of nothing more than how these swats would feel when, or if, Anne finally suggested she take down her pants. All these years without this particular kink answered, she was more than ready to bare her ass and plop it over her friend's legs for the swatting of her life.

Kathy stood, wiggled, maneuvering quickly so she was on her feet and standing to Anne's side in seconds.

"I really didn't wear the right panties for this," she said, looking down at her best friend. Unsnapping, and then unzipping her tight jeans, the voluptuous redhead shucked her pants down her thick thighs.

"Well, aren't they coming down too?" Anne asked and Kathy smiled as did Anne...and then peeled her tight white panties down her long legs. She stood there, her trim thin crimson path of hair slightly matted, her eyes downcast as she dipped her chin to her chest once again.

"Don't give me the contrite schoolgirl," Anne said and both women chuckled. "Or maybe you should."

With this, Anne sat back, Kathy scooted round to her side again, and Anne placed her hand on Kathy's lower back. Both women felt that instant magical rush when Kathy lay down again, her bare pelvis meeting Anne's bare knee, Kathy's bare butt high and ready.

"You're already a little red," Anne said rubbing her hand across Kathy's right cheek.

"Oh," Kathy squealed, trying to settle herself.

"You have such a beautifully round ass," Anne said, tickling her friend's bottom, running her fingers across Kathy's pale right cheek, and then her left. "Really, really round Kath."

"Fuck Anne," Kathy said, not even trying to hide her undulations then.

Not that either could know it, but neither woman had ever been with another woman sexually. Sure Kathy had been close a few times in college, but other than a few drunk late nights cuddling next to her roommates, and save for those fleeting thoughts Anne coddled over Angelina Jolie, this was the first foray either woman had taken in the world of homosexual encounters.

"This is gonna be good," Anne said and took her hand off her friend.

Anne and Kathy sighed in unison as they tried to calm themselves from what had just passed between them and for what was to come.

"Not too hard," Kathy said. "Remember my ass is bare."

"Like I'd forget," Anne chided, smiled, and raised her hand. "You gonna watch or are you gonna brace yourself?"

"Oh Lord," Kathy said, lying back down, her head dipped to Anne's calves.

"Let's start with an easy ten."

Neither woman said a word as Anne bounced her hand off Kathy's ass, again five high hard swats a side, but this time cheek-to-cheek. The rolling and hip shucking, the skin-on-skin retort, the heat and the musky scent, it was all heady stuff indeed. At the tenth swat, when Anne reluctantly stopped, she was trying with all her might to roll her hips closer to Kathy's side and Kathy was clutching both cheeks, pushing down hard into her friend's knees.

"Holy mother of fuck!" Anne shouted.

"Anne. Anne," Kathy sighed.

Still as they could make themselves, each woman teetered there on the brink of furthering this encounter, traipsing into an area well beyond just a good-natured, friendly answering of a curiosity. Kathy knew that Anne knew that given a few more well-placed swats she would most likely orgasm right there against Anne's knee. And Anne knew fully well that Kathy could feel her rolling ever closer while she smacked, trying to get her skirt pulled up even more so she might get some relief by pushing her pelvis into Kathy's side.

A silent half-minute passed as Anne stilled her hand on Kathy's heated right cheek and Kathy slowed her breathing and released her cheeks. The unspoken accord, the muted arousal enveloping the two, even the fall sunshine slanting through Anne's high living room windows—all these elements infused this encounter with a metered, cautious eroticism. When Anne and Kathy moved, they charged the very atmosphere around them; when they stayed still like this, it was almost as if Kathy was draped across Anne's lap in a non-erotic way, stillness seeming to hold the charged possibility of all of this at bay.

And the longer Anne and Kathy stayed still, silent, released, and relaxed, the longer they could avoid the question of *should* they continue.

Anne reached to her side then, stretching across Kathy. Kathy rose up to see what her friend could possibly be reaching for, but in her wildest dreams she never would have dreamed she'd see what Anne suddenly plucked from behind an 8x11 framed photo of Bill and the kids.

Worse than any implement she could have produced (and Anne wasn't sure she wanted to use anything on Kathy except her open hand) Anne extended her baby monitor as far as its chord would allow.

"Now, we continue," the mistress of the house said, flicked the monitor to hissing life, placed it down once again, and lifted her hand to continue swatting Kathy for whomever cared to listen.

The Corpse Washer

By
Jan Vander Laenen

"Classic is healthy, Romantic is sick."
- Goethe

Well, if one were to take this saying by the greatest German genius of all time *to the letter,* then I am a rather sickly being, because the more I advance in age, the more I catch myself to be a real, incurable romantic.

And yet, I have really tried to keep this romantic side of me hidden, perhaps because, in our cynical age, "romantic" is considered nearly synonymous with "ridiculous," and there is nothing that people nowadays worry about and indeed fear more than coming across as weak or, even worse, ludicrous. Furthermore, the term romantic is often still construed to refer to Death and ideas of death – ideas that are not exactly appreciated in contemporary society where we want to give the impression we are eternal and sickness and dying can be stopped and swept under the carpet... Oh, yes...

And so, I have had my frivolous rococo period, a period during which I plunged into the most diverse eighteenth century writers, and especially the writings of the Marquis de Sade and *Dangerous Liaisons* by Choderlos de Laclos, and well, sometimes, I perversely and falsely tried to pose as the character of Madame de Merteuil, or imagined myself to be even more sexually deviant than the aforementioned *Marquis*. Regrettably enough, with the help of my psychiatrist, I have had to come to the conclusion that manipulating, deriding, and lying are not really part of my character – no – on the contrary, I have been the one that has been swindled by others and driven in a tight spot – and that my sexual tastes could be called rather normal, or even sunny, never based on little power games, in other words, or with the danger of suffering permanent injuries, but just with the intention of giving and receiving healthy pleasure – with as many men as possible that, naturally, Don Giovanni was a precursor of the Romantic movement...

What I have retained from my "Enlightenment" period, is a life-long, total reverence for its music, and in particular that of Mozart, then, more naturally, a little flat which, in all its simplicity, seems to be done up like a miniature version of Versailles or Caserta or Amaliënborg.

And yes, I have also had a period during which I posed as an all but militant gay, a little in the American vein, perhaps. And naturally, I have been and shall, on the one hand, remain an ardent proponent of the gay movement and of human rights in general, but I am too well aware that there is still a lot of work to be done, and continue thus to do my little bit for our so-called "community." And on the other hand? Well, on the other hand, I continue to find that the saying "the world is beautiful because it is diverse" rings true, and would not feel really at home in a gay ghetto. And I naturally did enjoy my stay in the Castro district in San Francisco a number of years ago, but after a week or so, I was glad to be flying back to Europe. Because, well, the men there were naturally drop-dead gorgeous, with their facial hair and piercings and tattoos and their gym bodies; although it was a nice feeling to be able to knock about in a neighbourhood where men were the majority for once, I had missed the surreptitious, mucky, the secretive side, the sort of surreptitiousness, muckiness, and secretiveness that one can still find, in other words, in the stinking public toilets and stations and sex cinemas of European cities such as Brussels, Paris, or Madrid, for instance. Well, perhaps the American way of life is not really something for me...

...as was the case for that romantic Edgar Allan Poe for that matter, who may have emerged as the most illustrious representative of American literature, but who did not exactly have a high opinion of his predominantly profit-pursuing countrymen, and who managed to make a name for himself via Baudelaire's translations into French. Poor, poor Edgar Allan Poe, who saw his mother cough her last breath out when he was only two years old, and who then saw one young woman after another pine away for the rest of his life, so that love and death started to mean nearly the same thing, as can be gauged from the following verses:

I could not love except where Death
Was mingling his with Beauty's breath—

Death. Death! Have I been confronted with it myself? Oh yes, for I was born in Flanders, a region which, in spite of its Brueghelian reputation, seems to have been losing its *joie de vivre* more and more, where suicide statistics are not exactly pretty, and where the government takes pains not to publicise this fact. I was not yet eighteen when a good friend of mine, Rudy, threw himself under a train, for instance. I was not yet eighteen when another good friend, Jan, hanged himself. And I was not eighteen just yet when my then twenty-year-old brother–rich, athletic, intelligent, beautiful, and hairy and virile—ran into a post with his car at a hundred miles an hour. Poor, poor Guy, had you aimed a bit better, then you would have been dead on the spot, and have spared yourself some three weeks in semi-coma. Poor, poor Guy, who was the most beautiful of us and the darling of our parents, who taught me to masturbate, and about whom I may well have cherished incestuous feelings of being in love – how strange I felt when I greeted you for the last time in your brief life: because there I stood, the so-called weakling, towering over you who lay in your sickbed, attached to machines, with the hair on your head seared, your teeth smashed, your left eye torn out, and above all, an amputated lower leg. It did not do me any good to have seen you so felled, and the result of this early confrontation with death is that, as I grew older, I suffered more and more of a syndrome that I have christened "thanatitis," a rather morbid urge towards death. In other words, a feeling that I am constantly living under Death's wings, and that every action here on earth – and naturally, making love – could well be my last. "I could not love except where Death / Was mingling his with Beauty's breat—," Poe wrote, and given the loss of my brother, perhaps that applies a little to me too.

So far, so good. The title of this short story is "The Corpse Washer," and it is in his memory that I have now picked up my pen. In his memory? Yes, in his memory, because a week or so ago, Halal – corpse washer by profession, and an all but drop-dead gorgeous man, of such beauty in fact as to be well nigh fatal for me – dropped dead all of a sudden.

And yes, I can still remember where and when the likeness of this man graced my retinas... It must have been three months or so ago, on a beautiful September evening, in the Dada Café, a Flemish bar obliquely across my door, where I still go to down a few beers in the evening, usually alone at a table in the back room to apprise the other patrons that I have no wish to engage in conversation with them, and want to spend a nice little hour alone with my musings in my half-drunken stupor.

And what do I muse about? Well, don't laugh, but it is about serious subjects such as love, eroticism, art and death... Yes, and sometimes my ideas crystallise into a genuine aphorism, as the following, for instance, which on the evening before my encounter with my corpse washer, whilst reasonably drunk already, I scribbled on a beer coaster, and then put in my pocket: and life essentially boils down to creating one's own, personalised hereafter.

And what did I think of this aphorism the next morning, when, whilst nursing a hangover, I found the beer coaster on my writing desk next to my computer? Well, that I am probably an incredibly pious – and rather unlucky – man, perhaps because my little life has not exactly run smoothly up to now, and I am beginning to consider our earthly existence chiefly as a prelude to Paradise, although I will naturally spare no effort in the world to experience as many heavenly – read heavily erotic – moments, right here on this earth.

"...and life essentially boils down to creating one's own, personalised hereafter." Ah! Heaven! In my view, Heaven is naturally a real Heaven, a place where one never runs the risk of bumping into a member of one's family, in other words, and with streams of wine and other spirits, so that you can live in a constant state of stupor, without ever feeling the negative effects thereof, with such conversation partners as Mozart and Tchaikovsky and Boccaccio and Blixen, who know how to pull the most wonderful melodies and stories out of their sleeve, as if by magic, and with a *pineta* for their landscape, with a shore and a sea that is just a pinch sunnier and cleaner than the *macchia lucchese* in Viareggio, inhabited chiefly by dark-eyed specimens of the male species, ever ready for a romp, who naturally only speak romance languages – French, Italian, Rumanian, Spanish, or Portuguese, in other words. And who reigns in this Heaven? Why, God, of course, the most beautiful, most perfect, sweetest Man you have been searching for in vain your entire life, who will take you in his arms after you breathed your last too, for a never-ending story with the power of a continuous orgasm. Yes, indeed, and I, as a real melancholic type, can answer the prissy Catholic souls who reproach me for perhaps attaching a bit too much importance to eroticism, with a saying by Aristotle: "Melancholic types are, for the most part, obsessed by sex."

Ah! Heaven! God! The corpse washer, the man who must get us clean for our first appointment with God! Halal! There you were, on that sunny September evening, when I made my entrance in the Dada Café, sitting at the little table by the window, a mint tea in front you – there you sat in your drop-dead gorgeous glory, with your dark-bearded head, your limpid, black eyes that turned to look at me, and in which I thought I could read a certain holiness, the holiness of someone who is all too aware that we are here only temporarily, and can thus look Death straight in the eye; with an aura of blinding light around you; yes, yes, nearly a slap in the face of the ugliness that surrounded you, the musty floor and counter and tables of the bar, the unacceptably bad hard-rock music, the unfriendly barman, and the handful of half-drunk, unkempt Flemmings spluttering at each other – and my first question was, what in God's name is he doing here?

And this was exactly the first question asked by Evert, my neighbour and night nurse at Saint John's Hospital in the Rue du Marais, who happened to step into the bar, saw me through the open door, raised his arm to waive to me, saw my beautiful stranger through the window, and smiled at him with a somewhat surprised yet very polite nod. And my beautiful stranger smiled back, downed his last gulp of mint team, and with a supple gait and his well-built 1-metre-80 frame, dressed in bleached jeans and a white shirt with short sleeves, walked out of the Flemish watering hole, leaving me in the lurch!

And what did Evert have to say about my beautiful stranger when we bumped into each other on the patio of our building? Oh, that he too was amazed to see Halal, for that was his name, in the Dada Café, because this Halal was someone very discrete and very reserved; he worked as a corpse washer in the same hospital, but had no real contact with Evert or his colleagues; no one knew in fact whether he had a family or where he came from, and he always took his lunch alone in the canteen.

Needless to say, since that afternoon, my fantasies about Halal all but broke loose and that his likeness – I had seen him only once – has remained constantly before my mind's eye. And what kind of fantasies could these be? Well, they range from the most traditional to the most excessive. Supposing that I still wanted to make something of the life I still have left, I dreamed, for instance, that Halal was gay too, that I would meet him in a gay spot, that he would say *"je t'aime"* to me – the Flemish version *"ik hou van je"* has the contrary effect on me—and that we would live long and be happy together, and perhaps adopt children too. A more delirious dream was that I would see one of the erotic fantasies still on my wish list come true with him, to bonk so furiously together in public that we would end up in a police station for indecent exposure. For instance, we would first cuddle and strip and paw each other in relatively safe places, such as porno cinemas, peepshows, public toilets, and sex shops. But then things would get heavier and more frenzied each time, we would go and frolic about in our bare bottoms in the fitting cubicles of large warehouses, in passport photo booths at metro stations, and underground car parks, until finally, some prissy soul, preferably accompanied by innocent children, such as an infant teacher, for instance, would, completely out of herself, call in the Men in Blue.

My more morbid fantasies took even darker turns; he could, for instance, initiate me into the joys of coprophagy, very gradually, because taking part in a banquet such as the one in *Salò* has been no priority of mine, but I could have a look how a – his! – arsehole would open to press out a couple of brown turds – this was perhaps still a feasible sort of fantasy. Or, when I was feeling down, he could perhaps, for a quarter of an hour or so, the duration of Ravel's *Boléro*, anally penetrate and dilate me hard, so that in the end, with my permission, and with one thrust on the last dissonant note of the aforementioned composition, he would rip up my bowels to shreds.

Ah, Halal! What a vain fantasy; perhaps he was not gay at all, and would not want to raise a finger to me, so that my most romantic fantasy concerning him was of a suicidal nature. Because he was a corpse washer, the only way to get him to touch me was simply to end up as a corpse at his workplace in Saint John's Hospital. And oh, none other than him would then, for the last time during my presence here on earth–for I would then be shoved in the crematorium–would wash me, would close my eyes and mouth with a peaceful gesture, perhaps put some gauze in my nostrils, and then give my long body the once-over with soap; and perhaps a last shave, clip my rather bushy eyebrows, and touch my face up with some vermilion perhaps, and before dressing me–I opted to enter the Hereafter in a pair of bleached jeans, a simple chequered shirt, and sandals–he would still have to stick a wick up my arsehole, that organ that had provided me with so much pleasure?

And how should I do myself in? Oh, the plan to wind up bodily intact on Halal's wash table was simple: I would wait for the first freezing day of winter, to go out drunk, with a bottle of vodka and a last pack of cigarettes, and sit starkers out on my balcony at night, and freeze slowly to death, completely in line with "Let me freeze again to Death" from Purcell's "The Cold Song," performed so emotionally by AIDS victim Klaus Nomi. No blood or wounds or fractures, in other words, and I would not lock my front door, so that people would not need to force it, should anyone grow alarmed because of my absence.

Freeze to death! Andersen wrote his wonderful fairy tale "The Little Matchstick Girl" around this theme, and the first ice-cold day of the year, I am always slightly panic-stricken. My thoughts go out to the homeless in Brussels, and on my way back from Le Gémeau at night, for instance, I sometimes give one of them a bank note and beg him to go to a cheap hotel on the Place Saint-Géry.

Freeze to death! The first snow fell all too soon after that September evening when Halal came to rule over my thoughts. It must have been on 12 November, I believe. And as usual, I was sitting in front of my computer, working, that afternoon, glancing now and then at the falling snow, when an e-mail came in from Evert. It read as follows: "Dear Jan, first, sit down, if you are not already sitting in front of your computer. I know that you have had restless fantasies about the corpse washer, Halal, for a month or so now, but you never plucked up your courage to go and wait for him at the exit of Saint

John's Hospital to greet him or speak to him. Halal dropped dead suddenly, three days ago. The story making the rounds among my colleagues is that he still washed a gorgeous girl of eighteen or so, who had died of internal bleeding, and that he then—excuse my use of words—started zig-zagging down the Rue Neuve like a chicken with its head cut off, aimlessly, hysterical, screaming and yelling. When he reached the Eglise du Finistère, he fell to the ground and died from a heart attack. My excuses for the bad news. No one has come to claim his remains to date. I know that he came very close to your ideal. I was able to make a last photo of him with my digital camera, which I am attaching herewith. All the best, Evert."

And? And? Naturally, every letter of this zany romantic rhapsody of mine is pure fabrication, but the beauty of some men can arouse the most heavenly – and hellish – thoughts in me – and there can be no two ways about it... It's the only way that I can keep going. Amen.

Retribution

By
Billierosie

"I want your cock in my mouth."

"Jane?"

"Get your cock out, now!"

Silence on the other end of the line.

"I'm not in the habit of repeating myself. Get your cock out. What part of that didn't you understand?"

A nervous, male voice responded. "Jane, is that you?"

"As I said to you yesterday, who the bloody fuck is bitch whore Jane? Now get your cock out!"

A small smile tickled the corner of her mouth. She was enjoying this. Silently she blessed whoever had invented caller ID. Without it, she would have had no idea who the pervert was—the guy with the mellifluous voice who'd called her the previous day. The guy who'd wiped clean twenty years of hang ups and brought her to a shattering orgasm. It occurred to her she should thank him, but she wasn't going to. This was much more fun. Twice she'd called and got his voicemail. But that didn't matter; she'd discovered his name and profession, and through the wonder of Google she'd checked him out.

He groaned. "Oh God it's you, isn't it? Look I'm so terribly sorry. A stupid mistake. I dialed the wrong number. I'd meant to be calling Jane. It's her fantasy, you see. Getting a dirty phone call. It was meant to be a sort of late Valentine gift."

"So sweet," she said silkily. "But just fucking mention bloody fucking Jane one more time, and you're going to be in such trouble."

"So what is this? Blackmail? Got it all recorded have you? Or is it retribution?"

She chuckled. "Nothing so civilized. Do as you're told and get your cock out."

He laughed. "Aren't you supposed to ask me if I'm hard first?"

"Well, are you?"

"Yes. I am actually."

"Good. Okay, slowly unzip your pants and take out that big, hard cock."

God, she was getting wet herself. She hadn't realized talking dirty could be such a turn on. She could hear him breathing heavily on the other end of the line.

"If you're pumping your cock, you can stop right now." She surprised herself at how harsh she sounded. She fondled her breast, pinching the hard, erect nipple so it hurt. She felt a gush of fuck juices soak her panties.

Whatever he'd been doing, he'd stopped. His breathing quieted.

"Tell me about your cock," she said. "Describe it to me."

"Well, it's just a cock," he stuttered.

She'd obviously thrown him. He hadn't been expecting that.

"You're not feeling shy, are you, Marcus? Tell me what it looks like. Start with 'it's hard.' "

"Yes, it's hard."

"Are you looking at it now?"

"Yes."

"Tell me where you're sitting, Marcus."

"At my desk. In my office. I thought we were talking about my cock."

"Right now I want to get a feel for where you are. What sort of office? Modern? Traditional? You're an architect, aren't you? Do you have a ruler on your desk?"

"Right here."

"What's it made of?"

"Wood."

"Excellent," she laughed, delighted. "The old-fashioned sort. Always the best. Now back to your cock. Measure it for me. How big is it, Marcus?"

"Nine inches," he said immediately. There was an element of smug pride in his voice.

She laughed again. "I think you already knew that. You've measured it before, haven't you?"

"Y...yes," his voice sounded sheepish.

"That's okay, Marcus. You may have to be punished later. But right now we both want to talk about your cock. So it's long? Mmm, and thick. Would I like it in my mouth, Marcus?"

"Oh God yes!"

"I want to know what it tastes like. There are drops of pre-come on the end of it, aren't there? Just oozing from that little slit. Dip your finger in it and lick it off. What does it taste like?"

When he spoke his voice rasped. "Look, enough of this. I'm going to jack off now. Okay?"

"No, it's not bloody okay. Do as you're told and tell me what you taste like. Feeling a bit intimidated, are you?"

"No. Yes. It just feels weird you saying these things to me."

She gentled her voice. "Poor baby. Just tell me what you taste like."

Silence.

"Salty," he mumbled. "Kind of pungent."

"There, that wasn't so difficult, was it? Have you ever tasted cock before?" Her voice was sweet. "Don't lie to me."

There was a long pause. "Just once," he finally admitted. "A long time ago."

"At school?" she prompted. She realized she was fingering herself. Her index finger sliding between her wet folds. She brought her finger to her mouth and licked it clean.

"Yes. At school... And another guy, at university. After a football match..."

"And did you like it?"

"Yes."

"Did you swallow their spunk?"

"Yes..."

"Have you ever been sodomized, Marcus?"

"What!"

"You heard me. I'm going to sodomized you."

"I'm not bloody gay!"

"Well you're the one who said he liked sucking cock. Swallowing spunk."

"I never...I didn't. You're twisting my words..."

"Why do all men say that when they're losing an argument? You'll be telling me next that I'm crazy. Well, I tell you, Marcus, I doubt that there's a woman on the planet who hasn't been told by a man that she's crazy. I'm proud of being crazy; it's a badge of honor."

"I didn't mean..."

"Tell you what. This is going to be a lot easier if you strip off. I want you naked."

"But, I can't. There's a huge picture window here...I'm only on the second floor. Someone might see."

"Well you have got a point, I suppose. But frankly, I don't care."

She heard a rustling sound. Gosh, was he really stripping off? She felt immensely powerful. She felt an overwhelming need for penetration. Her finger slid into her cunt.

"Do you want to know how wet I am, Marcus? I'm fingering myself."

"I didn't know women got off on stuff like this."

"Neither did I. But I do, and I am. It's kind of great."

"I'm just going to put the phone onto speaker. You won't hang up, will you?"

She giggled. There was a note of desperation in his voice. "I might..."

"Back now," he said quickly. "I'm just taking off my pants. Damn this buckle. It always gets stuck."

She giggled again. She was going to make him wait a long time before she let him come.

"Are you naked?"

"Yes."

"Okay. You can stroke your cock. Just gently."

She could hear him drawing breath.

"Tell me how hard you are."

"Bone hard. I really need to come."

"No," she scolded. "Stand up. You and your cock."

"Oh God, people might see."

"Told you, I don't care. Are you standing?"

"Yes," he answered in a miserable voice.

"Oh come on. Do get in the mood. Would you rather I stop this now?"

"No, no, please don't stop. Please."

He was begging. That took things onto a whole different level. She touched her clit with her index finger. Her cunt clenched.

"Okay. I won't go. But first you're going to listen to me come."

She pushed three fingers into her cunt and thrust hard. She was hurting herself, but she didn't care. She stood up, one foot on the chair, widening her hole. Her finger clamped down on her clit and rubbed in little circles. The friction caused the tiny organ to send a sizzle of sensation through her cunt and pucker the tight bud of her anus. The orgasm had been building for some time; her pelvis pumped, and a gush of cunt juices soaked her hands. She cried out, a low bestial sound. She slumped down into the chair and was silent for some time, just thinking how wonderful it was to have that exquisite release. Then, guiltily, she remembered the man she'd left in a state of high arousal.

"Phew," she gasped. "Back now, Marcus. Sorry about that, but it was a good one. Did you hear me?"

"I heard you," he replied, somewhat petulantly. "When are you going to let me come?"

"I don't know," she said enigmatically. "First, I'm going to punish you."

"Don't you think this is punishment enough?"

"What? Not letting you come? I haven't even started yet. Pick up the ruler. Stand up. Now hit your cock with the ruler. Hit it, right on the helmet. Hard!"

"I can't," he said.

"Of course you can. Come on, one, two, three..."

To her amazement, she heard a crack and he let out a roar, and then a bellow. He'd done it.

"Well done, Marcus. Now again. One, two..." she trembled with anticipation. From the yelps and cries, it sounded as though he'd gone into a frenzy of flagellation. The surge of power she felt was intoxicating. She fondled her breasts and pinched her nipples. She rubbed her thighs together, realizing she was going to need to come again soon. The wild noises stopped. She could hear him sobbing.

"What does your cock look like now?"

He gave a low laugh. His breath rasped, "Red, swollen, bruised."

"You must have hit it very hard. Did it hurt?" she asked innocently.

He laughed bitterly. "It hurt like hell...but it felt ..."

"Good?"

"Yes," he sighed. "It felt good. What are you turning me into?"

"I'm not turning you into anything, Marcus. Just helping you explore your capacity for pain and self-control. Do you still need to come?"

"You know I do. PLEASE! Can I come now?"

"Patience," she said sternly. "Do you have any sort of lubricant in your desk?"

"Why?" he asked suspiciously.

"You must have some hand cream, or moisturizer. I know! One of those tiny cans of oil. Men always have them. It's for little machines, like when you take your computer apart and a screw gets stuck. See if you've got some in your desk drawer."

She could hear the sounds of objects being moved around. Shuffling papers.

"I've found some," he said sulkily.

"Great. Cheer up, Marcus. You'll thank me for this."

He did not reply.

"Go to the end of your desk and bend over. I want your upper body flat on the desk. Hold the sides with your hands. Is your ass sticking out nicely?"

"People can see me," he wailed.

She ignored him. But she was excited by the thought of him having an audience. She drew figures of eight in the folds around her clit; she was so wet.

"Reach behind you and trickle the lubricant into your ass crack. Start at the top, so it drips down over your hole. Put the lubricant down and pull your ass cheeks apart. Massage your fingers up and down your arse crack. Get used to the feeling; I know you think it's forbidden—taboo. But it's exciting too, isn't it? You're going to do something you've only thought about in your darkest fantasies. Now with your finger, massage the oil into your hole and slowly slide your finger into your hole just up to the first digit."

She could almost feel the heat of his concentration. She could certainly hear his heavy breathing.

"How does that feel, Marcus?"

"Tight," he muttered.

"Scoop up some more oil and try again."

She heard him gasp, and then groan.

"I'm in."

"Slowly push your finger in. Slowly. Tell me when it's all the way in." Her heart raced.

"Done it."

"Now, fuck yourself with your finger. How does that feel?"

"Weird," he said. "The stretching feeling's starting to feel strangely pleasant."

"Move your finger in circles; stretch your hole, make it bigger, so you can take more."

"Oh God."

"Try two fingers, Marcus. This is going to get better."

She could hear him sobbing.

"This shouldn't feel good, oh but it does. I'm fucking myself with two fingers now and it feels so good. Oh no. I'm coming. I'm coming and I can't stop."

158 | Retribution - Billierosie

She could hear the sounds of bellows and moans and crashes, so loud she feared for his safety.

"Marcus?"

"Oh, I'm sorry." He was weeping in earnest now. "I tried not to come. I tried so hard. But it was too much. Just too much sensation."

"It's okay, it's okay."

"I let you down. You told me not to come. Will you call me again? Please."

"No. I'm not going to call you again."

"But ..."

"Here's what I want you to do. Clean up the mess you've made while you're still naked. Lick it up, every drop. If you have an audience, that's too bad. While you're doing that, think about ways you can please me. Tomorrow, I want you to go to a sex shop and buy a pack of three butt plugs. Start with the smallest and work your way up. When you can get the largest one in your asshole and keep it there for twelve hours, then you can call me. Okay?"

"But what if I need to...?"

"Then the twelve hours starts again."

"Yes. Thank you."

"And get a video cam set up in your office, so I can watch you degrade yourself. I've got a wild imagination. I want to know that you're obeying me."

"Yes, Mistress," he said.

She hung up.

Empty Vessel

By
Shanna Germain

In the middle of my mother's long and exhausting funeral, my stomach starts to growl. Loud and long, a rolling rumble. Not a sound that should be heard during any kind of death service. Blatant enough that people look back. They look away again, of course, as soon as they realize that the protesting stomach belongs to me. Or they give me this long, quiet look, that tilt of their head that is supposed to convey, I suppose, sympathy. Or empathy.

After all, to all outside eyes I'm the grieving daughter. If I look gaunt and pale, if I haven't eaten for hours, for days, it is acceptable. Forgiven. Perhaps even expected.

Only Raul knows better. His look carries none of those expressions that people give when you are grieving, those perfect arrangements of lips and eyes that are supposed to make you – or themselves – feel better. He merely drops his hand to my skirt-covered thigh, tightening it so that his nails dig through my black nylons. The gaze of his dark blue eyes settles on my profile – I can almost feel the heat as he contemplates me – and somehow his thoughtful silence is louder than anything else in the room. Louder than the friends who break down halfway through their odes to my mother, louder than the *tick-tick-tick* of the continual clock, louder than my stomach even, although I can hear it, hear its groaning emptiness and everything that sound carries, more clearly than almost anything else.

"Tessa," he hisses so softly under his breath, raising one thick, black eyebrow. It is a question, but also not. It is a hiss of displeasure, not of disapproval quite, but surely of disappointment. A flutter of fear slides through my empty stomach, and I duck my head.

He slides his free hand into the pocket of his dark jacket, letting go of my thigh just long enough to unwrap a small piece of candy, the crinkle of the plastic burying the drone of the woman speaking at the front of the room.

I keep my chin to my chest, eyes closed, feeling the hard curve of the piece of candy as he pushes it to my lips. It smells sickly sweet, of strawberries and cherries and calories, and my stomach revolts. I tighten my lips closed, holding my breath until it is pounding behind my eyes, asking to be let out. His hand tightens into my thigh, nails pointed against my pulse until everything narrows into those tiny pinpricks of pain, until all I can feel is my blood heating up beneath the clench of his nails.

I exhale in a gasp, my head swimming with the new air, and Raul slides the candy between my lips. But the candy is on my tongue and Raul's hand is covering my mouth. Beneath the scent and taste of sugar, there is the scent and taste of him – heated flesh, the piney soap he uses, the metal of his ring. He never tastes of food, only of inedibles. Trees and stone and silver.

I feel people watching us – the daughter and her dark man, the one she won't marry, and does he have his hand across her mouth? And, somehow, worse, does he have one buried inside her thigh? At her own mother's funeral? Tsk.

And yet, knowing all this, all these things they can see and talk about, I still struggle on the pew, trying to break free. I attempt to force the candy back out of my mouth, but his fingers tighten.

"No scenes," he says, voice so low, so just for me, that I know he's leaning in, his lips nearly touching the curve of my ear. "Suck," he commands.

A sweet flood of sugar and flavor slides across my tongue, down my throat. Traitor, I say to my body, traitor. Resist. But it doesn't. It can't. It's been so long without food that it aches for it, needs it. Even as I tell myself that it doesn't.

I would sneak away, but Raul doesn't let go of my thigh. If I stood now, I know he wouldn't hesitate to tear my stockings from me, to pull me down into him with a forced growl that everyone could see and hear.

So I sit, and I think about my mother, and I listen to them say what a great woman she was, and I swallow down what Raul has given to my body.

It was a heart attack that killed my mother, at forty-six. No, not just one heart attack. This was her fourth in twice as many years. A bit of her heart sloughing off with each one until there was so little left. Her heart, I think, wasn't that big to begin with. She abandoned me when I was ten. And so very in need of a mother. She left behind a few things: a cat, overdue library books, a tub of blue cheese dressing, and three bags of chips. I stayed home from school for weeks, faking sick, waiting for her to come back. While I waited, I molded myself into the thing that I remembered of her: a woman with a cat in her lap, a book held open with one hand, the other hand constantly moving. Chips into blue cheese into mouth. Repeat.

She didn't return to my life until six years later, when I was sixty pounds overweight and she'd had her first attack. By then, I'd learned the clinical name for my ailment – binge eating – but it hadn't stopped me from eating and eating. My mother had called me from the hospital in a voice that I wouldn't have recognized even if it was healthy. I went there to see her, dressed in the one outfit I owned that I thought didn't make me look fat. She was huge, twice as big as when she'd left, her body barely fitting on the hospital bed. Her arms were mottled with cellulite.

"Doctor says I have to walk a lot, stop eating." Her voice hung, breathless and gasped. "So I don't have another attack."

"You're all I have, Tessa," she said, reaching a hand toward me.

I tried to touch her. I wanted to. But all I could see was myself, ten, twenty years from then, the way the fat had changed her face, her life, her love. I knew even then that I was a bad daughter, that despite everything, I should have forgiven. I should have taken her hand. But I couldn't. I could only fear what I was becoming and, in fear, run.

Binge swung to anorexia. At ninety pounds, I was on the verge of my own kind of heart failure. I understood intellectually what I was doing. I wasn't stupid. I knew it was all about control. All the things she took away from me, I would hold onto. Fisting around it. I understood it, but I couldn't stop it. It was the only thing that made me feel better, whole.

Men wanted me, and I fucked them, which made the world go away for a bit, but not really. I never came. I never closed my eyes. Too much letting go, those things. I knew how long I needed to fuck to burn off half a grape, how long I needed to blow someone to lose a quarter of a pound. I ate boys like butter, all those bodies and skin, not a calorie to be found.

It was Raul who saved me.

I know I'm not supposed to say that. I'm supposed to say, "I worked through my issues, and I've become a better, stronger person." I'm supposed to say, "I'm a recovering anorexic." I'm supposed to say a lot of things.

But mostly I try to say the truth. And the truth is that Raul saved me. The other truth is, if he ever goes away, I will be lost. Maybe admitting that makes me lost already.

I met him at a wedding, of all places. I was in the wedding party, and I felt good in my pale blue dress. Half an apple and a cup of coffee every day for weeks, and they'd had to take my dress in two sizes. I was dazzling in the aisle. And dizzy by the time it was over. I was ready to escape, to go home and lay down, away from all the noise and light and people.

A man with dark hair and midnight eyes caught me as I tripped on my way out of the church. Unlike everyone else, he didn't say, "Are you alright?" or "Do you need something to eat?" He didn't take my thin arms carefully in his hands when he righted me, saying, "I'm sorry, did I hurt you?"

No, he held me hard and tight, in a way that almost did hurt, but not as much I wanted it to, and he looked at me for a long time. Standing there on the church steps as everyone moved around us with swift, quick steps, carrying their glee in their hands like rice they could throw.

"Eat with me," he said. "At the reception."

I could only shake my head, my tongue a swollen, unused thing in my mouth. I hadn't planned to go to the reception at all. Anything with food was a scary place, a high place I might teeter and fall from. Break every bit of my resolve, become a heavy, unwanted creature with a dying heart.

"I'd like your company." His hand tightened along my wrist as he spoke. Was he scary? Not at all. He was powerful, though. Protective. I felt oddly safe inside the grip of his strong hands. Not like he wouldn't crush me, but that he could and would, that he would break me and free me. His eyes alone, the way they fell on me like dark weights, pinning me. I wanted to fuck him, to taste his skin, to make those eyes and that body fall down on me, trap me into nothingness.

"Yes," I said.

I sat beside him at dinner, toying with my napkin. There was food on my plate – salmon and vegetables and potatoes, a roll, a fat-laden pat of butter – but I couldn't touch it, couldn't begin to even think of it. I ripped my napkin into small strips, starting at one end and working my way to the other. Then I started crossways. Raul ate, watching me carefully.

"You don't eat."

"I do." I took a sip of water as if to prove it, the ice-cold liquid shocking my gums and teeth.

"You don't," he said. "But you will."

He picked a tiny piece of salmon up between his fingers. So small you could barely see it, but I smelled it, the way its oil slicked his skin. He put his fingers to my lips, and I pulled away, shaking my head, trying to get out of my seat.

His free hand caught the edge of my bridesmaid's dress. I could hear the fabric ripping, but still I didn't stop. I nearly turned the chair over in my haste, scrabbling away, caught finally when the dress wouldn't rip anymore. The rest of the wedding party went silent, turned to look at the tussle. My face burned and flushed. Air slid in, cooled the skin where the dress had been torn away.

"Sit," he said in a hiss. He wasn't going to let go.

"Put it down." He knew what I meant. The fish. He shook his head.

That was the moment. I stood, surrounded by a room full of mostly strangers, my dress ripped, my breath tattered, held by a man who watched me with nothing more than dark want in his eyes.

In that moment, I pulled away, hoping to drag the fabric out of his fisted hand and I ran out, dizzy, breathless, my heels the loudest thing in the place.

He caught up with me in the hall. I wasn't very fast, and I was confused. He backed me hard against the wall, put one knee up against my thin stomach to hold me there, and made short work of the rest of the dress, until he had a long strip of fabric in his hands.

He caught my hands in front of me, tied them fast and hard, the inside of my wrists touching each other so hard I could feel the veins pulse against each other. "Now, I'd like your company. But you'd have to eat something to sit with me. You choose."

He slipped away back toward the ballroom, leaving me tied, my chest heaving. I hated him. Presumptuous prick, my mind screamed. Asshole. And yet, I knew he was right. I knew that despite everything, I *needed* to eat. I *wanted* to eat. I was just so fucking afraid.

I went back. With my hands still tied in front of me. My dress half-off. My makeup smeared and streaked.

That walk across the room might have been the only brave thing I'd ever done in my life. The bride's face was a pale circle of confusion and fear. Other faces blurred between tears and exhaustion, and I was glad I couldn't see.

I sat back down next to Raul.

He didn't say a word, didn't even act like he saw me. Salmon rose to his mouth on the end of a fork, got eaten off. A wine glass was raised. Raul buttered a roll with his fingers–thick slabs of warm butter that coated it and covered it–and then he set the roll on his plate.

My face got hotter and hotter. The food smelled suddenly like heaven. I wanted it all. Every bit of it. I had to get away. I was stupid for having come back. I'd made a mess of things as I always did. I would go home, sleep. I would return to half-apples and cold tea. I could do it. I would. I would.

When I started to stand, Raul's greased fingers, sheened with butter – dropped beneath my hem and slid upward along the inside of my thigh. The heated scent of them kept me in my seat.

"Tell me," he said while he ate with the other hand, slowly, watching me with every bite.

"Nothing to tell."

His fingers slid the tiny string of my satin thong to the side, toyed with my bare lips. A rush of heat met his fingertips and my cheeks flushed hot and hard. My hands tightened inside the fabric that bound them, scratched at each other. I was dizzy from his touch, from the scent of the food, from the eyes that roved across me, from the clang and scrape of silverware around me as people went back to their dinners.

"Tell me," he said again. His mouth was full of salmon as he talked, his breath near my face a sea to swim in, his tongue a slippery fish that I wanted to suck.

I closed my eyes, felt my body waver. A single fingertip sank into me up to the first joint, wiggling against my slick heat until every nerve jumped and popped, my hips pushing forward against his touch.

He pulled away. The sound that came from my mouth was embarrassing, loud and groaned. I opened my eyes. He was looking at me, raising the finger that had been inside me, putting it to his lips and sucking my grease from it with as much relish as he'd eaten everything else.

I told him. The story of my mother, of me, of food. The short version. It sounded so stupid said aloud. Like I should have been smarter than that. But who can say the way things grow on us, and grow us? What small changes of body and brain will become our undoing?

He listened quietly, still eating, until I finished. Then he picked up a piece of salmon in his fingers again. This one bigger than the first. He brought it to my lips. The other hand returned to its place beneath my torn dress, fingers testing the waters between my thighs with barely-there strokes.

"I promise you," he said. "I will not let you become like her."

Was it so simple? Was I so see-through?

Yes. No.

The pink-red flesh touched my lips, slipped across the closed length of them. I could taste salt and sea and meat. My stomach growled and groaned, the wet sea between my thighs clenched in want, but I kept my lips pressed tight together.

He kept the slow brush of fish across my lips.

"Do you hear me? I will regulate everything you eat. I will feed you. And I will fuck you. And you will never, ever become like that woman. But you have to trust me."

I heard him. Of course I did. Who wouldn't? He was the first person who'd ever seemed to understand the fear. The need. Not the therapists. Not my friends. Not the other anorexics that I talked to in groups or in day-to-day life.

"Do you? Trust me?" he asked.

I raised my gaze to his, those dark depths of his eyes. I nodded.

He slid the fish between my lips as they parted in breath. Scraped his nail across my tongue as I swallowed. I sucked his fingers in a sudden hunger, groaning. Fingers slippery between both sets of lips, feeding me, ending my hunger. His other hand rose and fell inside me, until he was filling me at both ends, and I never ever wanted him to stop.

It worked. For so long, it worked. I trusted Raul and he fed me and fucked me, and I stayed healthy. Well. I didn't eat unless he told me to. All of my faith in one basket, as it were.

Until my mother called, on her deathbed, at the hospital. Family only in those last few days. So Raul wasn't there. He couldn't tie me up and fuck me. He couldn't sit across from me at a restaurant and feed me tiny morsels on a fork. It was just me and my mother, her bloated body. Why did I stay? I think I thought it would help me, if I forgave, if I let go, if I held her hand.

But no. I just... stopped. Didn't dare speak or breathe for fear of the things I'd say to her. Didn't dare eat. No. Not that. Not without Raul, not the way I wanted to stuff myself with cakes and cheese, with chips and ice cream and candy. I chewed my fingernails. I swallowed water to keep my stomach quiet. I watched her deflate and die, until she was a big nothing. And then I cried, but my tears tasted empty as water.

Raul waits until we get back to the house. He waits for that, at least. All this food, laid out on tables. All these people, stuffing their plates and their faces. Saying, "I'm sorry for your loss." I keep thinking they're talking about my weight, so I keep saying, "It's okay."

I can't help but watch everyone eat, and count calories. I haven't counted calories in years, but still it comes back with an ease that scares me. Fried chicken, potato salad, all the things that people bring to comfort themselves and each other.

"Tessa," Raul says as we pass the table. "You have to eat."

I know better than to deny him verbally, so I merely shake my head.

"I ate," I say. And I stick my tongue out to show him the overly red tongue, the leftovers of the candy he fed me.

He takes my hand and pulls me past the table into the bedroom. He slides the door shut, clicking the lock, and then leans against it.

"Are you your mother?" he asks.

"No. My mother's dead." You'd think it would hurt to say that, but it doesn't. There's something almost freeing in it, as though a stone – not a stone, a mountain – has been lifted from my life.

"And do you know why you're not your mother?"

"Because you feed me. Because you control me." It's the most true answer I know. But even as the spittle comes from my mouth, the hard crumbs of words, I know they're not true. I can't blame him. Want to, but can't.

"No, baby," he says. "Because you trust me. Because you're learning to trust yourself."

Is that true? I can't remember. I can't think straight. I think, somewhere behind the blur that is my mother and her big death, I think he's right. I had started to trust myself, to listen to my body. To take the things that nourished me into my body.

"Want do you want, Tessa?"

"You. I want you." I can already taste him on my tongue, down the length of my throat.

With little more than a groaned exhale, he comes to me and puts his hands on my shoulders, pushes me hard down onto the bed. He pulls my dark dress off in a careless yank of flesh and fabric. Seams tearing around me. His hands on my hips, he pushes me down to my knees with his hand in my hair. With his other hand, he opens his dark pants, fingers quick and rough as he pulls himself out, strokes himself to hardness.

"Eat," he says. And he doesn't give me time to answer. He just pulls me hard by the hair over his length, until I'm choking and gagging, trying to squirm away. "Eat," he says again and he jams me forward and back, a hard fast stroke that makes his tip hit the back of my throat. My knees burn from the rug and my breath comes fast through my nose, small huffs of air that whistle with every thrust.

He pulls me away, so that I'm panting and snarling. Swearing at him. And then he tilts my head up so I can see his eyes, all that dark desire coiling in those depths, all that love.

He lets go of my hair, takes a step back, and holds himself in front of me. His hand holds the base of his cock so that the dark length of it springs upright, clear fluid seeping from his tip.

"You choose," he says. And those words echo back to me from so long ago, and I shiver. Had I grown so little, come so far? My head is dull and achy from not eating, from crying, from resisting.

I open my mouth wide, like a baby bird, suddenly ravenous for every small taste. Raul smiles down at me. "Good girl," he says, and then he lifts his length in his fingers, letting the glistening head brush my lips.

My throat and lips and tongue, so unused, so abandoned, remember how to work. I suck him in, so greedy, so hungry, licking and biting his skin until he moans my name, his hand soft in my hair. I bury myself over him, suckling his length as hard as I can.

"Tessa," he says, all that pride and passion in his deep voice, and I feel my stomach tighten, not in hunger or pain, but in something new and nourished. He starts to come, and he pulls back like he always does, but I raise my hands to his hips and hold him inside me. I drink him down and he tastes of milk and tears, every drop as salty and sweet as life.

The Guessing Game

By
Mykola Dementiuk

It had been three weeks since he had last guessed correctly, but since she had only allowed him one guess a night and there was a limited number of colors he could guess at, the odds of hitting it correctly sooner or later should have been in his favor; but they weren't, and once again he had guessed wrong.

"Blue!" he stammered, thinking they had to be blue; it was time for blue anyway. Yesterday was white, the day before red, before that black, and it was pink four days ago...yes, today it would be blue! It had to be blue – besides, there was only one blue pair left in her dresser drawer, only white and red and black and pink ones in the laundry hamper, and since she only had two pairs of blue ones to begin with, they had to be blue!

"Blue!" he said, and no matter how logical and calculating his reasoning, still none to sure of himself. Because all the deductions, all the snooping through drawers, through laundry baskets, had led him to wrong conclusions before; he had counted, tabulated, sorted (and sniffed, clean ones and soiled) every pair in the house – there must have been over two dozen – and still for three weeks he couldn't come up with any pattern she followed to put on which pair with which outfit. Didn't a black dress with black hose and black shoes presuppose a black pair of panties? No, she'd wear green ones! Wouldn't white tennis shorts on a Sunday afternoon blend in perfectly with white panties underneath? Of course not, stupid! A shimmer of tiny red, circling, outlining, dipping into her highlighted attention-focused ass was the preferred style. So how could he ever guess what color she'd be wearing, or the logic behind it?

"Blue!" he gushed again, and winced. The look of disappointment was evident in her eyes, her mouth grimacing in disgust. He groaned, and felt his penis stiffen harder, more useless. But they had to be blue! They were blue this morning (he had peeked as she dressed) when she pulled on a pink skirt and went to work! But he knew they weren't; who the hell knew what color they could be? How many times did a woman change her panties in a day? Five? Six?

What was a pair of panties anyway? A strip of colored cloth, two, three inches of elastic, stretchable material—you could squeeze one in your palm and clutch it all day, like a sacred talisman or holy amulet, a good luck charm, take it with you wherever you went, to business meetings, to restaurants, to 12-Step programs, and who would be the wiser? They were practically invisible; he had never checked her purse, but he was certain if he had he'd find a few pairs in there too, in between the makeup jars, the lipstick tubes, the eyebrow pencils, the bulging wallets and checkbooks, the tokens, the brushes, the sales coupons, the tampons, the other panties...

Hell, the things were so tiny they could be shed and replaced in an instant! How convenient! Take them off on a hot summer day: just step into a hallway, lower the damp sticky pair, powder the ass and cunt, and step into a nice cool fresh pair of dry ones...

That's what the fucking panties in the streets were all about: everywhere you looked panties were lying on the sidewalk, in the gutters, on top of garbage cans, draped over fences, stuck on poles, everywhere you turned some cunning bitch unobtrusively tossing something invisible over her shoulder. Goddammit!! Hot sweaty cunts changing their wardrobes in the middle of the day in the middle of the street in the middle of the whole fucking city!

Of course they weren't blue! Who could possibly know how many colors they had already been that day? The fucking things changed by themselves every fucking minute of every fucking day! Like magic! Nothing up the sleeve? Nothing around the cunt either!

She sighed, looked at him sadly, and shifted her weight on the sofa. He scowled and clutched his crotch. It had come to this: his failure at guessing correctly at least gave him the consolation of peeking under her skirt to verify his wrong assumption, the frustrating consolation of gaping up her long nyloned legs, of eyeing the glimmer of unattainable moist flesh, of staring in disbelief at whatever-colored panties clasped the bloated bulb of her un-possessable cunt...

It was always the same scenario: she sat cross-legged on the couch, he knelt before her, guessed at a color, watched her uncross her legs, peered up her skirt, and spasmed in his pants; even if he guessed correctly and been rewarded with his first fucking in weeks, he knew he couldn't have gotten it up a second time. The anticipation, the fear, the anxiety probably brought on the force of his ejaculation as quickly and rapidly as did any abstinence or sexual stimulus under a female skirt. For three weeks he had creamed his failure at guessing correctly in his pants, and he was ready for another failed creaming right now.

She uncrossed her legs, the rustling whoosh of brushing nylons tearing at his soul and groin, and slightly pulled up a corner of her skirt, raising one leg up on the couch.

He gaped at her bare crotch.

"You fucking bitch!" he screamed. "You lying fucking whore!"

She smirked, and shrugged.

"It was almost a hundred degrees today," she said.

"You bitch!" he cursed, and stared at her bare pantyless cunt. (When did she shave that? But then, when had he last seen it?)

"It was hot," she shrugged, and smirked again.

He leaped off the floor.

"That's not fair!" he screamed. "You cheated!"

This was certainly outside of the ground rules of their guessing game. This was cheating; he knew, and so did she. They agreed there'd be no trickery of any kind—no arguing or bickering over color-shades or tints: blue would always be blue, not seaside marine; red was red, and not majestic scarlet; purple would be purple, and not evening magenta; pink pink, and not pussy blush, or whatever the cunt-clothes-catalogs she got in the mail called it. And if she wore tiger-stripes or colored spots of polka dots, any color on the panty he guessed at was valid to take in the entire panty and he won. And got laid. But pantyless? And hairless crotch? This was outside the rules. This was cheating. And it wasn't fair!

"You cheater!" he cursed, and leaped at her. "I'll give you panty pussy, you cunt, you whore!"

She giggled as he unzipped his pants and was in between her legs, fast; she didn't even resist, and wanted him, pulling him in her. It had been three weeks for her too! And he was in, and out, and in, and out, back, and forth, back, and forth, in, and out, her ankles on his shoulders, her ass at his balls, his cursing mouth (Bitch! Whore! Pussy! Cheater!) spitting at her, grunting, yelping, teeth and lips (Oh God! Yes! Fuck me! Oh! Cock!). She screamed, he yelped, they came, and he collapsed atop her heaving chest, her legs falling down his arms but circling around his ass and waist and holding him in...

They gasped into each other's ear; they kissed.

Maybe the guessing game had gone on too long. He gently stroked a breast; the cup under the blouse seemed stiff. Was it new? Blue? He leered. Since the blouse was red, her fashion logic probably called for green. He asked. She smirked.

"Guess," she teased.

He guessed; she frowned.

"Guess again..."

You Awake Ahead of the Alarm

By

Oatmeal Girl

You awake ahead of the alarm, the sun knocking on your face, the drapes deliberately left open the night before. She is curled up at the end of the bed, the obedient thing, the light-weight extra blanket partially covering her nakedness, a pillow tucked under her head, her arms wrapped around your feet. She snuggles in closer and moans with pleasure.

You awake ahead of the alarm, the sun knocking on your face, the girl snuggled close, warm flesh melting into warm flesh. She presses her face into your chest, foolishly seeking comfort from the source of her degradation. But all that matters to her is that you are her Master. Whatever you do to her, whatever you demand, she accepts as a gift. She presses herself in closer and moans softly with pleasure. You thread your fingers through her tangled red hair and use it as a handle to raise her face towards yours. Well trained, she opens her mouth and presents her tongue. You kiss her softly, deeply, your body coming closer to consciousness in her mouth, before sinking your teeth into her lip.

You awake ahead of the alarm, the sun knocking on your face, the girl snuggled close, pressing her back into your chest and her bounteous bottom into your crotch. You are hard, your cock having awakened long before the rest of you.

Somehow, in the course of the night, she ended up spooned against you, your arms around her, her front so conveniently positioned for torture. Like a boy driven to pull the wings off elegant butterflies, your fingers inexorably move to her nipples. A normal man would have fondled her breasts, cupped them, circled his hands gently around them before pressing gently in on the hardening nipples. You are who you are. Like a rabid lobster, you grab each nipple, pinching, digging your nails in, and then twisting them as far as they will go, and then one notch farther. She gasps, jerks, and screams, jolted out of her illusion of intimacy into the reality of an intimacy much deeper than she had ever known before you snared her. You reach down. She is as wet as a saturated sponge. You thread your fingers through her tangled red hair and use it as a handle to pull her head to the side before sinking your teeth into her neck. You leave them there, feeling the blood pulse beneath your mouth, feeling the desire pulse in your cock, wishing your teeth were sharp enough to pierce the artery. You want to feed on her. She moans with pain and pleasure, grinding her ass back into you.

You push her on her back and throw yourself on her, crushing her down into the bed. You lower your mouth to hers, barely giving her enough time to part her lips and present her tongue. You kiss her, and then pull back and slap her face, ordering her to soften. She cries out from the slap, she's not used to being slapped, she whimpers slightly and struggles to relax in the middle of panic at having displeased you. She has no gradations of grief at disappointing you. Any failure feels like the end of the world to her.

You enjoy the luxury of a long exploration of her mouth. She gives herself with pleasure, she can't help feeling pleasure, while fighting the urge to return your kisses with the fierce passion that you know is crying for release. You smile inwardly at her frustration. You always know it is there.

She struggles beneath you, gasping for air. You castigate her for wriggling without being ordered to do so. You pull yourself off her, relocate to the side of the bed, and haul her over your knee. You spank her hard, for fun more than anything else, for the pleasure of her screams, for the pleasure of her tears, for the pleasure of the darkening blush that spreads across that delicious butt.

Damn, but you're hard.

You glance at the clock on the bedside table and sigh inwardly. There is never enough time. Moore will be unbearable all day if you turn up late for tee time. He'll be teasing you enough as it is, you don't want to give him one more excuse to razz you. Not that you don't have plenty of ammunition to use against him, what with that bitch who took up residence and made off with his balls. What desire can do to a man...

You end the spanking, and give her time for the sobs to subside. You love the way her belly shakes against your lap. You examine the welts that remain from the caning you gave her the night before. Beautiful. Not to mention the initial you scratched into her flesh with the ragged end of the wooden strip you use as a cane. You love the feeling that courses through you when you mark her.

Enough. You rise up off the bed and toss her onto the floor. She starts to scramble to her feet, but you stop her with one word.

"Crawl."

"Please, my Master." She sounds so plaintive. "Please, Sir, may I pee?"

"Of course, my pet," you say, enjoying the little sigh of relief that escapes her lungs. Your testicles pulse at that small, breathy sound. She crawls the short distance to the bathroom, she crawls on her forearms and knees, giving you an unobstructed view of her inviting pussy and well-defended butt hole. You follow behind her and kick open the bathroom door when she foolishly, naively, tries to close it.

You stand there at the door, pointedly watching, as she pulls herself up onto the toilet seat and tries to relieve herself. You see a look of panic cross her face. You know she is too tense. You know she can't let it go. You know she is horribly embarrassed. You make a show of leaning against the door jamb. You're not going anywhere.

She blushes. You hear her make a little hissing sound to herself. She starts to look down. You order her to look you in the eyes. She raises her head, looks you in the eyes, gives you her soul, and continues her imitation of a small boiling tea kettle. You see it in her eyes before you hear the spigot open. She smiles. She exults. She has given you what you demanded.

"Good girl."

She is ridiculously pleased with herself.

You push back the shower curtain and start the water running. You send it up to the shower head and order her into the tub, giving her butt a gratuitous smack on her way in. She turns back to you and grins.

Sharply, abruptly, as if displeased, you order her to face the wall opposite the spray.

"Spread-eagled," you bark. "Push those tits into the wall! Arch your back! Bring that lovely ass up as high as you can. Let me see my property. All of it!"

You know exactly what she's expecting.

But she won't get it.

Not yet.

You watch her struggling to hold the position exactly the way you described it. Her eager willingness to do whatever you want makes you hot. She is so fucking easy to manipulate.

It clearly takes a moment or two for her to identify the hot stream of liquid that suddenly strikes the small of her back and makes its way in a rivulet down her ass and into the crack between her cheeks. You only wish you could have seen her face when she realized it was urine.

And then she surprises you. She doesn't flinch. She writhes a little, she presses her tits further into the ceramic tile, she arches her back even further, she raises her ass even higher, she tilts her head back, you almost think she's going to cum, and then—

"Thank you, my Master," she says in that damn breathy voice. "Thank you for marking me, thank you for claiming me, please, Master, pee all over me, i am your pet, i am your poet, i am your whore, i am your toy, i am nothing except what you want me to be. Degrade me, hurt me, fuck me, share me... i am yours and that is all that matters."

You come up close behind her and fuck her ass.

Tits for Tat

By
Jude Mason

Shaking his head, Peter *Tat* Jackson wondered what had possessed him to go along with her request. He thought he knew her, but as it turned out, she knew him a whole lot better. She'd managed to gain control of their relationship somehow and that both mystified and excited him.

Looking down, all he could see were gigantic tits – his.

Tat knew he was young, virile, and handsome in a dark foreboding way. He also knew deeply that he was God's gift to whoever he fancied at the moment. Hell, he'd been told often enough by an assortment of both men and women, and he wasn't stupid. He listened and believed.

The trouble was, Tat had secrets. One he'd never shared with anybody and thought he never would. Then, four years ago, he met Susan MacKay and his world changed completely. It took some time, but he grew to care for her, and then trust her implicitly with anything and everything. A year after they met, he found it almost easy to reveal his deepest, darkest fantasies to her. Susan had seemed to relish each new detail, every juicy tidbit. It wasn't until nine months ago he began to worry that perhaps she was a little too interested, a little too under-standing, and possibly a little too perverted.

Lying on his back in their king-sized bed, those soft mounds rising majestically from a chest that used to be fairly flat yet well muscled in a very masculine way. The tip of each tit was crowned by a luscious red nipple surrounded by an areola, the circumference of which would be large enough to fill the palm of any woman he knew.

Woman, what woman would ever want him again? What woman would ever look at him again without laughing her ass off?

Fuck! What have I done?

Rolling over, he pushed himself up and sat on the edge of the bed. It took him a moment to get his balance. Still unused to the *weight* of them, he tended to tip forward and had nearly toppled over several times. He couldn't see past them – hadn't seen his toes, or other appendages, in months. Carefully, he leaned forward, peering down between those giant melons. No luck, but he couldn't be disappointed. Deep in the depraved depths of his lustful heart, he thought they really were spectacular.

"Tat," came a stern yet hushed feminine voice from the doorway. Susan had taken to calling him that after she'd spotted the small tattoo he had on his lower belly. It wasn't anything outrageous, just a small upside-down heart with a delicate, elongated nipple pointing at his belly button. He, of course, couldn't see that either. Not without a mirror.

He looked up at her. Dark haired, voluptuous yet tiny compared to his six-feet-two, she still turned him on, no matter what she'd talked him into. "Lady Susan," he replied, using the pet name she'd suggested a couple of years ago while they were in the throes of passion. She seemed to enjoy it very much, and it completely turned him on. "I'm awake, come in."

"Jeeze, Tat, every time I see you, I want you again."

His cock twitched and lengthened, sliding along his inner thigh. "You say the nicest things." The head of his cock jerked against his thigh and he reached down for it. Fingers slipped around the shaft, he gently massaged himself.

"Have I told you, your tits look amazing?" Susan eased out of her robe, her lovely, firm tits suddenly pointing toward him. "Move up, put your back to the headboard."

He looked down again, and had to agree with her. He adored big tits – the bigger the better. That was part of his secret, the innocent part. He absolutely loved gigantic tits, wanted to bury himself in them or mound them around his face and be smothered.

Before he met Susan, he used to dream about sliding his cock, which in those dreams was always so much bigger and so much harder, between a pair of enormous boobs. He'd come in his sleep, shuddering and groaning, like some adolescent having a wet dream. The few times he'd actually found women with the right sized breasts, he'd scared them off with his over exuberant pawing and not so playful nipping.

But now, thanks to Susan, his lover and his Lady, he had his very own set of succulent mammaries. Adding to his pleasure, she seemed as enamored with them as he was, and had spent hours caressing and nibbling on them since his surgery.

"Now!" Lady Susan snapped her fingers, regaining his attention.

Scooting up the bed, he leaned against the headboard and placed his hands on the bed at his sides. A moment later, she straddled his thighs, her wet, pink inner flesh grazing the base of his cock. She leaned forward, pressing her soft skin against his, her breasts flattened against his.

"Mm, this is nice," she murmured in that deep steady voice he'd heard so many times before. She'd accept no denial or slackness, and he'd give her no reason to punish him. She raised her face, her eyes meeting his. "Hold me. I want to feel your strong arms around me. Press our tits together."

Tat's heart fluttered. He pulled her close, mashing their breasts together. Her nipples felt like tiny marbles digging into his tender flesh. "May I kiss you, my Lady?"

Looking deep into his eyes, she smiled. "Yes, of course you can, just be careful and don't come." Closing her eyes, she pursed her lips and waited.

He took a breath and pushed down the urge to turn her on her back and take his pleasure. He leaned down, brushing his lips against hers, savoring the minty toothpaste taste of her breath in his mouth. Tongues met, entwined and battled with the other, only to dip deeply into the other's mouth, wanting more. He slid down her back to the curve of her ass, cruelly tempted to cup her butt cheeks and pull her astride. Instead, he eased her even closer, mashing their tits together. The pressure of Lady Susan's smaller mounds flattened against his much larger ones felt amazing, and he wanted it to go on forever.

The sudden sensation of her hand wrapped around his cock nearly sent him gasping over the edge. "Play with my tits, please, my Lady," he breathed into her mouth, needing to have her hand off him.

"Oh yeah, babe." Sitting back, she peered down at his chest. She relinquished her grip on his shaft only to reposition the splayed talon-like grasp on his soft, white boobs. Her hands weren't nearly big enough to contain them, but when she dug her fingernails in and squeezed, he swooned with pleasure.

Feminine he might be from the waist up, but he still had the strength of a man. He fought that strength with every fiber, refusing to move her, to drag her hands from his tits, to fuck her like the animal he knew he was.

"Like that?" she whispered, her mouth contorted in a wicked smile. She twisted her wrists, dragging each firm mound in a semi-circular motion.

"Yes, oh fuck." He shuddered with frustrated lust. His nipples tensed into hard knots of sensation. Each time she moved her hands, his taut nipples dragged over her palms and sent tiny shocks straight to his balls. He bit his lower lip to keep from screaming for more. His cock pulsed between them, its swollen head slick with pre-cum.

"Don't you dare come, Tat." Her wrists twisted the other way.

He grunted, shocked at the bite of her nails – a welcome diversion. He focused on them, imagined them driving into the head of his cock and dragging around the rim. *Wrong! Dumbass*, he chastised himself.

"No, my Lady, I won't. Not until you say." His voice was like gravel dragged across pavement. He loosened his grip on her and forced his thigh muscles to relax. His cock pulsed, the tender flesh of its head tapped against her soft lower belly.

"Even if I do this?" That wicked voice nearly drove him that millimeter too far. The firm grasp she had on his tits vanished.

He looked down just in time to see one of her hands wrap around the base of his shaft. With a grip tight enough to make him wince, she held his prick head away from her belly.

"Well?" She flicked the tip of his manhood with her free hand. "I'm waiting. Do you think you can hold off, even when I do this?" She stroked his length from balls to rim and used her thumb on the crown. Dragging it across the slit, she smoothed the oozing drops of pre-cum around.

"Oh my Gawd, please, Lady Susan." He gyrated his hips, unable to stop and not really sure if he was trying to come or escape her tormenting fingers. Shards of bright ecstasy jolted his prick into a wild dance of need. He wanted to come, yet, he wanted to obey his lady.

Susan again held his shaft tightly and flicked the crown.

It focused him, it tore at him, and he bellowed, "Yes, I can hold." He thought that was the end of his cry, but the words, "Please, stop," followed an instant later.

He blinked up at her, his lips clamped tightly together, just in case.

"Please stop?" She continued her teasing caress, dragging the skin up, and then down his shaft, pressing the ball of her palm against his balls on each down-stroke. "But, you like this, don't you, my pet, my Tattooed lovely?" She tilted her head and jiggled her tits in his face.

"Yes, yes, I love this," he agreed hastily, desperately.

"Yet, you ask me to stop." She pouted, but her eyes still had that mischievous look he adored, dreaded.

"I'm so close, you're driving me crazy."

"I know, isn't it fun?" She brushed the palm of her free hand over Tat's nipple, forcing a guttural moan from him.

"Yes, it's fun. Fuck, I can't stand it. Please, Lady Susan, can I come?"

She scowled at him, but didn't slow her torturous masturbation, nor the delicate brushing of her hand over his nipple. "But I haven't driven you crazy enough yet."

Blood pounded in his ears so hard he wasn't sure he'd heard her right. *Do I dare ask her again? Can I hold off for a few minutes longer?* His hips jerked forward, driving his prick through her fist. His balls churned. "Please, oh fuck." His cock swelled and his balls climbed higher. The skin covering them tightened, crinkled. "Please, Lady Susan, I'm begging you." He looked into her eyes, his own near tears and asked, "Please, let me come now. I can't hold off. I thought I could, but it's impossible."

"Pinch your nipples." Susan demanded, withdrawing her own hand. She reached down and cupped his balls. The smooth skin gripped his, a stray finger delved back between his thighs until the tip rubbed over his tightly clenched anus.

Tat raised his hands, fingers automatically finding the elongated nipples and latching onto them. He inhaled, and then squeezed.

Just as his heart lurched from his self-stimulation, Susan increased the pace of her masturbation. Mouth as dry as the Mohave gaped, a tongue no wetter dragged across parched lips in a useless attempt to moisten them. He groaned. Sweat poured from his pits and his brow. He shivered.

"Come for me, my sweet slutty Tat." She winked at him and pumped his cock hard.

"Yes, my Lady," he croaked and closed his eyes. Clenching his glutes, he thrust his hips forward. Nirvana enveloped him as his orgasm tore its way from deep inside. He grunted. A burning stream of cum exploded from his cock and he pinched his nipples tight again. He twisted them, dragging a moan of pain-filled pleasure from him as he spewed his second shot.

He looked down and groaned. Susan looked as if she were masturbating her own cock. Two bodies, one cock, four tits to cream over. He was in heaven.

Another ribbon of cum shot up and splattered on her right tit. It was the last; all that remained was the shuddering ooze of his climax pouring over her fingers – that and the back and forth pinching of his nipples.

"Messy, very messy," Susan mumbled when she released his shaft and lifted her fingers to her mouth. She sucked on them, licking at the white cream clinging to each digit. A sultry smile and the lashing of her tongue made his cock pulse. Even though he'd just climaxed, she had a way about her that made him want her again.

"You can let those go now. Let me see how red you've made them." She leaned forward and pressed her lips to the sore nubbins. Tenderly, she licked his nipple, the wetness cooling the dull ache of his harsh treatment. She lavished one and moved to the other, humming a low tune as she worked.

Exhausted, his thoughts free, he remembered their first date. Arranged by a cousin, they'd met at a dance and hit it off right from the word go. He'd adored the dress she'd chosen, red, tight to the waist, but with the deepest scoop neckline he'd ever had the pleasure of seeing. Her amazing tits, her nipples clearly visible, were like magnets drawing him in. He couldn't take his eyes off them. They'd danced, and he'd drooled. He found out later, she'd loved the attention he paid to her, and her breasts. She'd also adored how he'd jumped to her every whim.

They hadn't fucked, but they'd both wanted to. Two nights later, after an evening of talking and teasing each other to distraction, they had. A glorious fucking it had been. She'd demanded he please her with his hands, his mouth, and finally his cock. She ridden him, her warm sweaty thighs tight against his sides controlling their pace while she pressed his hands to her tits, encouraging him to twist and squeeze the enormous mounds. She screamed her climax when he'd given each nipple an especially sharp stab with his thumbnails, her own dagger-like talons buried in his elongated nips, and her cunt clenched around his spewing shaft.

When they'd collapsed together, she chastised him for not asking her permission to climax. It was as if a light had come on inside him. He'd become excited all over again.

They'd lain, side-by-side on his king-sized bed, and talked some more. She'd confessed her love of everything to do with breasts – her own and others. She also told him how she'd fantasized about having both, tits and cock, to control and play with. Little did he realize how his life would change in the coming months.

"Hey." A sharp dig in the ribs brought his attention back to the present. "You okay, Tat?" She slid her hands down his sides, and then back up to his chest, his tits. She cupped the sides of them, pushing them together.

"Yeah, I'm okay," he managed, but still hadn't completely recovered. "Gimme a second, please. Gotta catch my breath, my Lady."

Pushing off him, she looked down at the mess they'd made and chuckled. "Okay, you catch your breath. I'll go get a washcloth." Bouncing off the bed, she sidled toward the bathroom, giving her hips an extra sway.

Tat ogled the delicious plump ass until it disappeared from view. *Yeah, she's got a great ass too.* But, it was the knockers that drove him wild. Just thinking about them made his cock twitch.

The night she'd asked him to tit fuck her, she'd come right along with him. It was like she had a clit on each nipple, and every time he tugged on one, she'd spasm. When he'd reached back and slid a finger into her sopping wet pussy, she gushed all over his hand. That's when she told him about how she wished men had tits. She wanted to play with them as they fucked.

Reaching up, he tugged on his own, and shuddered. His cock pulsed even harder and began its slow rejuvenation. He reached for it.

"Hey, hands off my property," she said from across the room. She stood in the doorway to the bathroom, a damp cloth in her hand.

Snatching his hands away, he gazed up at her and smiled. "I was thinking about us, and this is where it got me." He sat up and spread his legs. Even though he couldn't see his cock, he felt it growing, reaching toward her.

"You know better than to touch before asking."

She was right. It'd been a rule for some time and he knew what could, would, or might happen if he forgot. His little ploy at playfulness had failed, as he knew it would. "Yes, my Lady. I'm sorry." And he was, surprisingly. During sex play, she often let it slide, but the sex was over, for him at least.

"I love your tits, Tat." She strode ahead, stopping at the foot of the bed.

Tat glanced down at his gorgeous, monstrous tits and had to agree. "Thank you, Lady Susan, I love them too."

"I love that cock too." She crooked her finger, beckoning him forward. "Bring my cock to me."

Tat scooted forward, until his legs dangled over the edge of the bed, his toes on the floor. Leaning back, he placed his hands on the covers and spread his knees. His tits rolled across his chest, the nipples again taut with excitement. What was she going to do?

"Excellent," Susan said in that stern tone he adored. "Shift your shoulders, make your tits move."

While he rolled his shoulders, she leaned forward and took his slumbering cock in hand. When her fingers wound around the shaft, it throbbed to semi-hardness.

"Lie back on the bed," she instructed as she worked the smooth flesh of his cock up and down the shaft. "Hands behind your neck."

The growing excitement made catching his breath difficult, but he didn't care. Flopping back, he thrust his hands behind his head and waited, eager for her to decide the next move. The wait seemed eternal. Finally, she touched him, or the cloth did. She wiped him down, cleaning the essence of his cum from his belly and thighs. Apparently satisfied, she removed the cloth, but her hand continued its careful stroking. His breathing had time to calm, the heat faded from his face. His prick stiffened to its fullest. Her pace became more insistent and he fought the urge to thrust into her palm. He flinched when a fingernail dragged over the crown.

"This belongs to me." She emphasized her statement with a sharp slap across the head of his cock.

He never saw it coming. He grunted and drew his knees together, or tried to. She'd positioned herself between them, denying him that defense. "Yes, my Lady. Yours, all yours."

"These too." She grasped his balls with her free hand and held them tight.

"Yes, yes, yours, my Lady." Fear threatened to break his voice. He tensed the muscles in his belly, readying himself for the pain he dreaded, loved.

"I haven't come yet," Susan said in a husky whisper. Her fingers tightened on his balls. As he squirmed and forced his groans of pain down, she added, "It's my turn."

"Yes, Lady Susan. Please, may I use my mouth on you? My hands? Whatever you want?"

"Keep your knees wide. I want to see a hard cock." She twisted his ball sac and squeezed.

"I will. I will, Lady." His inner thighs trembled with strain. His nipples tightened.

"I'm timing you. Take too long and you'll pay later." She released him, leaving his cock to flop over his belly, his balls to rest between his thighs. "Keep your hands behind your head. Just your mouth."

"Yes, Ma'am."

Susan climbed over him as he lay breathless and trembling, straddling his hips, and then forcing his tits between her legs as she clambered higher. When her knees pressed against his ears and her pussy hung suspended mere inches from his mouth, he knew he was in for a treat.

She simply lowered herself. No preliminaries or niceties, she just spread her knees wider and settled her juicy wetness onto his mouth. Her ass came down on Tat's huge round breasts, one cheek per tit.

"Oh yeah," Susan moaned when he took her luscious labia between his lips and suckled on them as he would the most delicate of treats. He flicked his tongue across them and when his mouth filled with her juices he was on the right track. He pried her open with his tongue, delving for that hard little nubbin at the apex of her slit. Finding it, he twirled his tongue around the tiny bud.

Her fingers wove into his hair. Pain tore at his scalp and he would have yelled if he'd been able to escape the grip of her thighs. The rich smell of her filled his nostrils. The succulent sweetness of her cunt came close to overwhelming him.

In a strange kind of retaliation, he devoured her. His teeth slid across her labia, his tongue pushed into her clenching hole. He dined on her nectar, savoring every drop. He pressed his nose against her, stabbed at her with his tongue, and grazed the taut pearl with his teeth.

She trembled, her thighs tightened, and her fists in his hair clenched. He thought she'd pull it out, but he didn't care.

"Yes, yes, do me," she cried, and he strained to obey.

His cock pulsed, its stiffened shaft tapped insistently on his belly. He would have smiled, if he could, but he had much more important things on his mind. She'd shifted forward, cutting off his air. He knew he could move her, but he didn't. He took her clit between his teeth and gnawed carefully on the nerve-filled morsel. He pushed his tongue into her, fucking her with it and hoping she'd cream before he had to breathe.

She shuddered wildly, coming, her thighs tensed, and then relaxed. She bounced, her ass flattening the giant mounds of his tits and driving the last of his breath out.

His mouth filled with her cream and he swallowed it all. Her spasms fed him, and the sight of her above him made his blood race.

She collapsed moments later, falling to her side on the bed. He lay gasping, trembling, and smiling like a fool.

"Thank you." He looked at her, hair askew, face flushed and her eyes glazed.

She gazed back at him and smiled. "What?"

"Just, thank you." He rolled onto his side, careful to keep his hands behind his head. "I never thought I'd be here, like this." He looked down at himself. The smooth flesh was mottled, his nipples puckered and tight.

"Slut," Susan murmured.

Tat smiled. "Yes, I'm a slut. Your slut."

"Yes, you are." She rolled closer and reached down. He felt her hand on him, sliding over his lower belly until it reached his prick. "A horny slut."

"For you. Always."

Her smile got bigger. "Yes, always." She took his rampantly rigid erection in her hand and gave it a couple of slow easy strokes. "I think it's time we talked about a collar, possibly another tattoo."

"Collar?" he asked, secretly thrilled at the prospect.

"Yes, a collar." Her hand tightened around his – her – shaft. "Maybe a small one that fits around this. You're mine now, just as I'm yours. We belong together and I've got the resources to take care of us both."

Tat smiled. He was home.

The Only One

By

M. Christian

The buzz was angry in her ear. She felt sad at that. The pain was hot and glorious, and she felt sadness that the only way her mind could relate to it was a bee – buzzing angrily in her ear. Dani tried to speak, from her ozone-level high of her endorphin rush, to tell Her that she wasn't seeing faery lights, the godhead, cosmic strings, or hot leathersex and chrome. But the gag got in her way. She arched her back instead.

"Look, Bill, she likes it."

The buzz worried her hip, at first an irritation, and then a burn. Dani was aflame. They were at the letters now, the typewriter blocks that were the heart and soul (and reason) behind the tat, behind being strapped (arms at sides, legs pressed together) on the hard, leather-covered bench. The letters being tattooed onto her were the all and the everything: PROPERTY OF MOE. RETURN POSTAGE GUARANTEED.

The letters were why she was there.

Stars danced in her eyes. With a little imagination the buzzing bee went back to its hive and her field of vision expanded out to became a ballroom, where she danced in the clouds of her euphoria. Dancing was something special and hidden; it made Dani soft and small again. The hardness of her skin, her attitude, and outward affect made the vision seem a lie, a tall-tale: a biker chick pretending to be Barbie. The unkempt hair, constant T-shirt, utility (not fashionable) jeans made her out hard and steel. But behind her eyes a much younger girl was dancing with her first boy. She was wet between the legs then too.

She was little Dani, dancing in her mind, lying on a hard, leather-covered board, being tattooed. She tried to smile but the rubber ball in her mouth made it difficult.

"I think she's asleep."

"Give her work," recommended Bill, the tattooist.

The thought of the first voice's owner made her extra warm. Her Goddess's voice. Her owner's voice.

Her mind, in its liquid endorphin ocean of pain and distance, slipped back to a hazy memory of their first contact; the day the Goddess smiled upon her and made her come.

The memory was distorted and frayed from too many replays, too many examinations. What had they really said? Had this strange woman who had suddenly started talking to her at the bus stop really smelled of boot polish and sweat? Had they then talked further, over hot, and then warm coffee, till they couldn't stop touching one another? Had this strange woman, encased in leather like some ambulatory cocoon, calmly taken a single strand of her hair between red-lacquered nails and pulled Dani unprotesting into the fetid, sickly sweet garbage of a nearby alley? And once she was there had she been kissed deep and long? Had a shiny-red nail really dipped down below the belt-line of Dani's jeans, and come up wet? Doubts and more doubts.

One thing was certain: hot love that afternoon. Love mixed with a stern voice, hard hand, and – like an insect mating call that leads to a frightening sting of revelation – handcuffs on her wrists, face between her legs, and a coming that had left her dizzy, raptured, and worshipful.

Soon after (Days? Weeks? Months? How long?), a simple request to her from out of one of those evangelical orgasms: "Do it for me." A simple request. Compared to the scalpels she'd been introduced to, the flailing whips, and alligator clamps, the pain would be nothing – a breath of cool air on her hip, she was assured, and nothing more.

But now the pain was a flare on her side. The tattoo was burning. The pain starred her eyes suddenly, flicking her out of her memories, into the here (on the leather-covered table, in the upstairs of the tattoo parlor) and the now. Above her, a single bulb in a faded (once white, now cream) shade. The gag was snapped out of her mouth. The air of the parlor was thick with dust and smoke. She wanted to cough, but had forgotten how – all she could do was swallow the pain.

Through it, a slow eclipse. Then the shadow resolved itself, and her Goddess spoke, "Time to get to work."

Above her, legs parted, and in between shiny desire (and the earthen smell of smoldering cunt), her Mistress spread her second lips, positioned herself carefully, and slowly sat.

A face, no matter how wide open or receptive, is not the best of seats. With her submissive's nose pressed hard and pointed into the smooth channel between asshole and cunt, Moe twisted right and left to use the butterfly fluttering tongue to her best advantage. Early on, when the lips met face, the tongue had tried to probe for best effect. Moe quickly ended that with a practiced nod to Bill, the tattooist, to hold for a second, and then, gripping one of Dani's little points, a nipple tight with excitement, between thumb and forefinger, Moe twisted.

Muffled by her ass and cunt, Dani's squeal was suppressed. Then, beyond belief, a sharpness, a snake in her cunt. She'd been bitten. A smile crossed Moe's face. The first time. The prize of having something different, unique, made her jingle like Christmas bells. The first time anyone had bitten her. Dani's apologies were unspoken and earnest: a simple lapping of her juice. The twist had come as a surprise but the message had been clear: *I won't try and please you, for that is presumptuous, so I will just lick and you will please yourself off my tongue*. Lesson learned.

Moving herself as best to use the tongue, Moe found herself coming, a hissing orgasm that made her legs turn to pudding. With a smile on her face, she pressed down hard (the tongue was deep in her wetness, clit forgotten), and blissfully rode the orgasm.

And, as she came, she thought: The first bite. The only one.

The cunt, the heavenly wetness, the sweet mask of her Goddess's ass, lifted off Dani's face. She blinked, licked her lips, and breathed deep. The breath was short; the needle started buzzing again.

She was so lucky, so special, to be here, to have this done. To join her Goddess, to have her Goddess joined to her. Moe had chosen her. Moe had picked her to be her slave – to be a prized possession, a glittering trinket on an empty shelf. The ego rush made Dani's head swim against the pain. Then the needle really went to work. It tickled, it burned – the pain became central to her being, important to her. It swelled in her, pushing against her soul, making itself known, making demands. Making her unspeakably horny.

The pain played with the awful need of her cunt (when she arched her back, the suction her leaking pussy made held her tight). The experience of the burning needle and the hornies made her head ache, her stomach crawl. Madness or orgasm?

She couldn't make up her mind. Couldn't they see, the tattooist and the Goddess, the way her clit was dancing. Couldn't they see that little fleshy dancer, wiggling and writhing like a worm on a hook? Touch it, for God's sake. Someone, please touch it!

She would've screamed, except the gag was back in her mouth. She arched her back, as much as she could (which wasn't much as exhaustion, gravity, and finely crafted restraints pinned her butterfly to matt board).

Somewhere below her, beyond the gentle rise of her stomach, a beautifully trimmed silhouette, Moe dispensed justice. Her thunderbolt was a firm slap to her mons. The shock ran through the tissues of her pubis and reverberated against a glass-hard clit. Stars lit up Dani's brain, water poured out of her (she was sure) as she drained in a torrential downpour of one long, steaming, fluid orgasm.

As consciousness slowly returned, as the dreamless fog rectified itself into that same damned lightbulb, a face, The Face, "You did good, Property." Moe said to her, "You did good."

Tucked in bed, bandage covering PROPERTY and the rest on her hip, the Biker-Barbie-doe was asleep on her ballroom floor. Dani was asleep under her comforter, the firm never-never land of sleep around her, face pressed into a futon, cheek wet with drool. The party was over, sleep was called for. She embraced the prescription for afterplay recovery.

But the needle wasn't quiet, it didn't sleep. Sitting on the leather bench, Moe got the addition to her tat in stern silence. Well, not too stern, for a smile twisted her Mona Lisa grin. She was thinking about the nip to her cunt (it still stung). The only one. The Only One.

Moe smiled as she got the tat – on the side of her head, just over her ear, under a small patch of hair (shaven by Bill, with quick, practiced waves with his chrome straight-razor). When the doe awoke, she'd see the bare skin, see the addition to the existing and know the truth. That was the fun, that was the glory. The thought of it made her loins tingle. Quietly, softly (she was being tattooed, for Christ's sake), she started to masturbate.

Moe smiled. The Only One. And really, really smiled, as Bill turned four tick marks into five on the side of her head. The Only One.

She laughed at that.

Author Bios

Billierosie lives in a pretty village in England. She doesn't fit with village life, certainly not the Women's Institute. This is Billierosie's first published story. She loves the theatre, art, film, books, and all things eccentric. Billierosie plans to have fun and stay young, writing pornography.

M.Christian is an acknowledged master of erotica with more than 300 stories in such anthologies as *Best American Erotica, Best Gay Erotica, Best Lesbian Erotica, Best Bisexual Erotica, Best Fetish Erotica*, and many, many other anthologies, magazines, and Web sites. He is the editor of 20 anthologies including the *Best S/M Erotica series, The Burning Pen, Guilty Pleasures*, and others. He is the author of the collections *Dirty Words, Speaking Parts, The Bachelor Machine, Licks & Promises, Filthy, Love Without Gun Control*, and *Rude Mechanicals*; and the novels *Running Dry, The Very Bloody Marys, Me2, Brushes*, and *Painted Doll*.

Mykola Dementiuk is the author of the novels *Vienna Dolorosa, Holy Communion, Times Queer and others*. His novella, "My Father's Semen" in *Cruising for Bad Boys* came out last June 2009. Also a sexual novella about *D Day*, "Dee Dee Day," will be out this Christmas 2009 from eXtasy Books. See his web page for more information: www.mykolademeniuk.com.

Shanna Germain believes in dark, dirty sex that strips away our walls and turns us into windows. You can read her lust-filled work in places like *Best American Erotica, Best Bondage Erotica 2, Best Gay Bondage Erotica, Best Gay Erotica, Best Gay Romance, Best Lesbian Erotica, Blood Fruit: Queer Horror, Dirty Girls, X: The Erotic Treasury* and at http://yearofthebooks.wordpress.com.

Oatmeal Girl is a submissive, Jewish, bisexual, feminist baby boomer, who regrets she can't brag to her mother about having a story accepted for publication. "My daughter, the pornographer?" Not likely. This story was an assignment for her sadistic master, to whom it is dedicated. Poems, stories, and more at submissionandmetaphor.blogspot.com.

Ralph Greco, Jr. is an internationally published author of short stories, plays, essays, button slogans, 800 number phone sex scripts, children's songs and SEO copy. Ralph is also an ASCAP licensed songwriter/performer and Internet radio D.J. He lives in the wilds of suburban NJ, where he attempts to keep his ever-expanding ego in check.

Theda Hudson burns up the pages with lust, leather, and latex, brims over with juicy bits in *Best Lesbian Erotica 2001, 2002 & 2006, Cthulhu Sex Magazine,* Amatory-Ink.com, lucreziamagazine.com, *Hot Blood XI: Fatal Attractions, Best of Women's Erotica 2007, Who's Your Daddy, Got a Minute?,* and *Hot Lesbian Erotica*. When she's not hard or wet at the computer, she's a factotum, artist, and intuitive.

Kane was born in Bristol, England in 1981 and now lives with her partner and four cats in a big white house. Her stories are inspired by personal events, snatched conversations overheard on public transport, and pure imagination. She loves writing as the opportunity to create a world with words in which other people can be absorbed and excited.

Jan Vander Laenen lives in Brussels, Belgium, where he works as an art historian and translator (Dutch, French, and Italian). He is also the author of eight collections of short stories, plays, and screenplays which have attracted keen interest abroad. A romantic comedy, *Oscar Divo*, and a thriller, *The Card Game*, are presently in the hands of a competent producer in Hollywood, while his short fiction collections The Butler and Poète maudit are eliciting the requisite accolades in Italy. His most recent publication are the tales "A Glass of Cognac" in *Bears: Gay Erotic Stories* (Cleis Press), "Epistle of the Sleeping Beauty" in *Unspeakable Horror* (Dark Scribe Press), "Fire at the Chelsea Hotel" in *Best Gay Love Stories 2009* (Alyson Press), and "The Stuffed Turkey" in *Best Gay Erotica 2010* (Cleis Press). He credits Karen Blixen and Edgar Allan Poe as his literary influences.

Multi-published Canadian author, **Jude Mason**, writes in a variety of genre stretching the boundaries at every opportunity. She has work in print with Cleis Press, Phaze and Total E-Bound to name a few. Jude also has dozens of e-books available and a few in audio. Check out her website: www.my-haven2001.com.

Jean Roberta teaches English in a Canadian university and writes in several genres. Over 70 of her erotic stories have appeared in print anthologies. This includes three other "Dr. Athena Chalkdust" stories: "Splitting the Infinitive" in *Best Lesbian Erotica 2001*, "My Debut as a Slut" in *BLE 2005*, and "The Placement of Modifiers" in *BLE 2009*. Jean Roberta's *Obsession*, a diverse collection of fourteen stories, is available in print and downloadable form from Eternal Press. Her opinion-piece column, "Sex Is All Metaphors," appears every month on the site of the Erotic Readers and Writers Association. More information is available here: www.JeanRoberta.com.

Jerry Rosen is a writer who is perpetually interested in how people use their bodies as a vehicle to reveal their secret fantasies and desires, their most voluptuous dreams. His fiction focuses on the wishes, lies, and dreams we tell ourselves, and others, about who we are and what we really want. He's currently writing a screenplay.

Jason Rubis lives in the Washington, DC area. His erotic fiction has been published in many anthologies, including *Like Clockwork* (Circlet Press), and *Needles And Bones* (Drollerie Press). His story "Barefoot" appeared in *Best S/M Erotica 2*.

Craig J. Sorensen's short stories and poetry have appeared in print anthologies by Alison Tyler, Maxim Jakubowski, and Rachel Kramer Bussel, in magazines internationally and various Internet publications including Clean Sheets. He is currently writing an erotic novel based on his experiences stationed at a Military Intelligence Unit in West Germany at the dawn of the 1980's.

Cecilia Tan is the author of many books of erotica and hundreds of short stories. Recently she has been found writing erotic romances like *Mind Games* and *The Siren And The Sword*. Her erotic high fantasy, The Prince's Boy, is running as a serial at circlet.com from 2009 through 2011. Find out more at ceciliatan.com.

Sharon Wachsler's work has lately appeared in *Femmethology, Periphery, Bed*, and *Frenzy*. She has a tattoo named Ingrid and used to have a variety of symbols shaved into her hair. Her most recent "reading," "'Sexual Language and Behavior' as defined by Massachusetts law," helped defeat a ban on "adult establishments" in her 900-person town.

Xan West is the pseudonym of an NYC BDSM/sex educator. Xan's "First Time Since," won honorable mention for the 2008 NLA John Preston Short Fiction Award. Xan appears in *Best SM Erotica 2, Best Women's Erotica 2008 and 2009, Hurts So Good, Sextime*, and *Leathermen*. Email Xan at Xan_West@yahoo.com.

P.M. White dressed as a woman on two occasions, both times for money. While he enjoyed the whiskey he drank while wearing a dress, the panties and hose were too tight. Next time he wears a dress, White said he plans to go bare-assed and drink even more.

Other Great Erotica Titles from Logical-Lust

The Cougar Book

Cougar women are smart. Cougar Women are sexy. Cougar women are *hot*.

Read this scintillating collection of Cougar stories edited by Jolie du Pré and featuring the best erotica writers around.

Includes an introduction by the original *Cougar* – Valerie Gibson.

$13.99 US, £9.99 UK, $6.99 eBook download

Swing! Adventures in Swinging by Today's Top Erotica Writers

Whether you are a swinger, think about swinging, or just interested in reading about it, *Swing!* has something for you!

Another acclaimed collection by Jolie du Pré and featuring the top erotica writers.

$14.99 US, £9.99 UK, $7.99 eBook download

The Award-Winning Kielan series

Time Currents, the second book in the Kielan short story series by Brenna Lyons, is the **2010 EPIC eBook Award Winner for Fantasy Erotic Romance.** You too can experience the Kielan phenomenon with *Time Currents* and *The Lady's Lowborn Lover,* with more series stories still to be released!

$1.99/$2.99 eBook downloads

Bittersweet

2010 EPIC Award Finalist.

Stories of tainted, bittersweet erotica, written in a literary, engaging, style by debut author Amber Hipple.

Not all love stories have happy endings. Be moved by the cycle of wanting to be wanted and the pain of wanting too much.

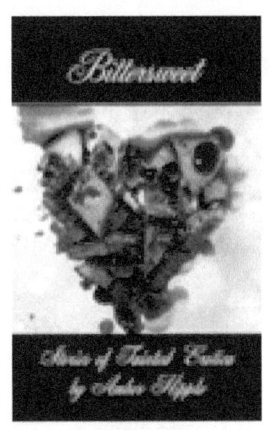

$7.99 US, £4.99 UK, $5.99 eBook download

Got Men?

Author G.A. Hauser takes the reality show phenomenon a step further in her original m/m erotica story, *Got Men?*

The set up for the big 'reveal' on the reality show Got Men? is more than just a simple decision. It's about taking a risk. The producers of the show want the subjects to take that chance, because to them, ratings mean everything.

$15.99 US, £8.99 UK, $5.99 eBook download

Future Perfect – A Collection of Fantastic Erotica

Speculative erotica at its best from author Helen E. H. Madden, from the adventures of a sexually obsessive superhero to the best orgasm you'll ever have – at the end of the universe.

Helen takes erotica to a whole new level in this astounding collection!

$11.99 US, £8.99 UK, $5.99 eBook download

Scouts

An overpopulated space station threatens to separate two young loves. At any moment, Challers Dizen could find himself conscripted by the Fleet and forced to become one of their lethal, over-muscled Marines, while Valka Parl could be taken away by the gluttonous Merchants. Their only hope to stay together is to join the mysterious Scouts.

$12.99 US, £9.99 UK, $5.99 eBook download

Messalina: Devourer of Men

Eva Cavell is a woman with an embarrassing secret...

A tenure-track instructor at a private Denver college, despite desperate attempts to maintain control, Eva's world is spiraling into chaos. As emotional pressures build inside her, an explosion is imminent. Will she ever be able to live her life how she wants and without shame?

$12.99 US, £8.99 UK, $5.99 eBook download

Find our books at www.logical-lust.com, Amazon, Barnes & Noble, and all good online retailers!

Logical-Lust Publications

"Taking the Reader Down a Different Path"

www.logical-lust.com

Award-winning titles, and award-winning authors

www.ingramcontent.com/pod-product-compliance
Lightning Source LLC
Chambersburg PA
CBHW022100170626
46808CB00002B/531